I0548834

Seducing Sir Gwain
The Gwain Series, Book 1

by

Shari Dare

Published by
Melange Books, LLC
White Bear Lake, MN 55110
www.melange-books.com

Seducing Sir Gwain ~ Copyright © 2014 by Shari Dare

ISBN: 978-1-61235-888-8 Print

Cover Art by Stephanie Flint

To my friend and Ouija partner. Without her Gwain would never have been conceived in my warped little mind.

Chapter One

"Gwain." The pointer on the Ouija board spelled out the name Denise Hopkins had only read about in *King Arthur and The Knights of the Round Table.*

"Are you Sir Gwain?" her friend Lydia Thompson asked.

The answer was an immediate, *"No, but I am named for him."*

Both women giggled. They had been playing the spiritual game on their lunch hour for years, always taking little stock in the answers the mystical board gave. The predictions rarely came true and when they did it was certainly like a blind squirrel finding a nut.

Without asking the questions, the pointer spelled out a message. *"I lived in Scotland."*

Gwain was different from any spirit they had ever contacted in the past and they wanted to know more. Usually their spirits were women who predicted things like grandchildren that never materialized and jobs that were nonexistent.

"I knew you in 1470."

Denise and Lydia exchanged surprised glances. "Who did you know?" Denise asked.

"You," came the answer.

"Were you my husband?" she questioned, winking broadly at Lydia.

"You were my brother's wife and we were lovers."

Denise and Lydia pulled their hands away from the board at the same time.

"I don't even want to know any more about this guy," Denise declared.

"Do you think he really was your lover in a past life?"

"Of course not, but it was creepy."

Lydia closed up the box and put the game away. They'd decided to play this afternoon to try and see what their future held. Denise had just lost her job and was coping alone since her husband of forty years had died suddenly almost a year earlier.

"It would be fun to have a phantom lover," Lydia said when she returned to the kitchen. "Can you even begin to imagine how much fun it would be to have an affair with a handsome Scotsman?"

Denise began to laugh. "How handsome can he be after being dead for five centuries?"

"You know what I meant. He could materialize as a young man and sweep you off your feet. You know what they say about life on the other side—everyone there is thirty and gorgeous. It could prove interesting to have a ghost as a lover."

The two women again had a good laugh over the idea of ghosts materializing in the bedroom. It didn't take them long to move on to other subjects of conversation, like what they thought was going on at the place where Denise had worked for so long, since she was no longer there.

After a light supper, Denise sat down to watch TV. *Just my luck, they're showing Braveheart tonight. Of course it's just a coincidence.*

Mel Gibson made a dashing Scotsman, leading his men into battle. Her favorite part of the movie was when the Scots mooned the British army, which also proved to Denise that they wore nothing under their kilts.

With the end of the movie, Denise turned off the living room TV and went into the bedroom. Since she still didn't like going to bed alone, she switched on the bedroom TV and set the timer.

Law & Order SVU played out the plot of this evening's show, while Denise fell asleep, secure in the knowledge the TV would shut itself off at eleven when the show ended.

Dreams took over when her conscious thought ended. In the dream, a beautiful young woman wearing a Scottish plaid appeared. Her long red hair accented the color of the plaid perfectly.

"Davida, come with me and we will be together

2

forever. I do not want to wait any longer to make you completely mine."

"Oh, Robert, you know we cannot do this. As much as I love you, I cannot disappoint my uncle. He has been planning our wedding to coincide with the fall festival."

"Then my darling, let me taste your nectar."

Davida pretended to run from her beloved only to have him catch her. Once they were on the ground together, he pushed her skirt high above her hips and gazed at the fire-red curls that guarded her womanhood.

"Take me quickly and quench the fire that burns within me," she pleaded.

He lifted his kilt and she saw his cock, hard and ready to be embraced by the velvety folds of her cunt. As soon as he entered her, she moaned with pleasure.

Denise heard the sound of rain pounding against her bedroom window. To her disappointment, the noise produced by the storm dissolved her dream. She knew it had to be late, because the TV was dark and silent.

The erotic dream made her hungry for self-satisfaction. She cursed Fred for dying and leaving her alone with her sexual hunger. She could no longer wake her husband and ask him for a hand-job to make the longing go away. Many years ago their sex life had faded to nothingness, but he was always gracious enough to accommodate her, even if he couldn't get it up to give her the full pleasure she desired.

Alone, she decided to start with manipulating her breasts and tweaking her nipples the same way Fred had done for all the years of their marriage. She tried to slip her hand up her nightshirt only to find her body encased in a long cotton gown. The realization brought her to full awareness.

The gown didn't belong to her and neither did the bed. Certain she was still in the midst of a weird dream, she pulled the hem of the nightdress up until her hand rested on the mound of hair at the juncture of her thighs. To her surprise, the curls she felt were as tight as they had been when she was young. They certainly weren't the sparse ones of a

3

postmenopausal woman. Out of curiosity, she slipped her hand into the warm damp valley that hid her woman's soul. The bud of desire grew under her fingers the way it had grown when she was first married and discovering just how wonderful sex really was. *If this is a dream, I don't want to wake up.*

It is no dream, Denise, the voice of the woman in her dream said. *I am not strong enough to withstand the future that the soothsayer has foretold. I have begged her to help me change places with a future incarnation of myself. From now on, I am Denise and you are Davida. The old woman has assured me that you are much stronger than I, and the events that are about to unfold are ones that you will be able to withstand.*

"That was strange," she said aloud. It surprised her to hear a Scottish brogue to her voice. Almost convinced that she had changed places with the beautiful maiden of her dream, she reached her hand further up her nightdress. She smiled to realize that a flat stomach had replaced her middle-aged paunch and her drooping breasts were now full and youthful with very large nipples. They certainly were different from the nipples of her breasts. Just touching them, she knew that any man who caressed them would give her pleasure beyond her wildest dreams. Every fifty-something woman's dream was to regain the body of a younger woman and still retain the wisdom of age. For some unknown reason, she had been brought back to the past and she intended to enjoy every minute of the adventure.

"Davida," a woman said, as she entered carrying an old-fashioned lamp. "'Tis your wedding day, lass. Your uncle has sent me to fetch ye."

The light that illuminated the room told her that the voice of the woman from her dream had been true. Somehow she had changed places with the beautiful young woman. Denise did not know why Davida thought she could not endure being married to the handsome Robert. What she did know was that no matter what happened, from this moment on, she would be Davida and live her life to the fullest. If Robert was half as good as he had been in her dream, things could be interesting. She certainly wouldn't be dull old Denise who enjoyed almost forgotten sex with her husband, but only in the missionary position. She would experiment and show the man some love tricks that she knew he'd never

4

dreamed possible.

As soon as she threw off the covers, she immediately felt the chill of the damp manor house where Davida lived. What she wouldn't give for a well-insulated house with central heat at this moment.

Somehow she knew that the woman who had come to wake her was a servant. Not knowing exactly what year she'd been transported into, she allowed the woman to help her bathe in the tepid water she had poured from the ornate pitcher into the matching bowl. She longed for a shower, but realized that she was now living in the past and that a shower was something reserved for future pleasures.

The woman scrubbed her with a rough cloth. Just having it rub across her nipples made Davida feel as though she would have an orgasm at any moment.

When the woman was convinced her charge was completely clean, she started to help her to dress. It amazed Davida at the sheer weight of the garments she was forced to wear. Even the wedding dress with the long train she'd worn forty years ago didn't weigh this much.

It's no wonder these women aren't fat. They work it all off carrying around these clothes.

By the time she was escorted to the dais that had been erected in the courtyard, people were already feasting and enjoying the games. In the distance she saw Robert. She recognized him immediately from the dream that had brought her to this time and place.

"My friends," said an older man who she assumed was her uncle, as he assisted her to sit beside him. "Today my niece will be given in marriage to Robert Brier."

Robert walked toward the dais, a smile on his lips, while Davida, as everyone here knew her, looked at the older man beside her. If he was her uncle, where was her father? Why wasn't he the one giving her away in marriage?

With no answers forthcoming, she looked back at Robert. The memory of the dream she'd had made her wet with anticipation. Marriage to this man could definitely be exciting. She found she couldn't take her eyes from his kilt and kept imagining the cock that rested beneath it. A "dangly man part" was how she had seen it described in one of the many historical novels she had read. With this man it was far from dangly, especially when it stood at full attention. Just thinking about his cock made her even wetter, and she squirmed with anticipation of the night to come once they were man and wife.

"I challenge your decision, John Burke. Davida was promised to me when she was a babe. Did her father not even tell his brother of this?"

"Who are you?" John demanded.

"I am Charles of the McGowen clan. My father entered into this agreement on Davida's naming day. She is mine and has been for the past twenty years. It has taken me a long time to find where she was taken when her father was killed."

Davida felt her heart begin to break. This man was almost ten years older than she was and ugly as sin.

"Her uncle has given his blessing to our union," Robert protested.

"He had no right to promise her to you," Charles shouted.

"Then prepare to die," Robert declared, drawing his sword in challenge.

Davida sat transfixed, unable to take her eyes from the fight taking place in front of the dais. It was no wonder that the former resident of this body didn't want to live her life any longer. "Why don't you stop them?" she pleaded.

"If McGowen is right, his claim on you must be honored. If Robert hadn't challenged this man..."

"You could stop this," she continued.

"What has begun cannot be stopped until one of them is declared the winner."

And the winner gets me. Why did I ever think historicals were so romantic?

Before her eyes, Charles struck a blow that ended Robert's life. Suddenly the man who had dominated her dream and propelled her back into this time period lay dead at her feet. The life that Davida had planned was suddenly changed forever.

"As the winner, I claim the prize," Charles declared. "My men await me with a wagon for her belongings. I expect them packed while the priest marries us. I want to be on my way as soon as possible."

Davida shuddered. In front of her Robert lay, his lifeless body no longer filled with a bright future. Beside him stood Charles. *Did this chick whose body I now inhabit know about Charles? Is that why she told the soothsayer to help us change places?*

The marriage ceremony was short and to the point. There was no kiss from the groom, no receiving line, and no wedding cake smashed into her face. Instead, she was taken immediately to the room where she had awakened hours earlier.

The same servant who had awakened her came in to help her pack her toiletries. "I cannot believe that…that man killed Robert," Davida lamented.

"He wants ye, lass," the woman she now knew as Anna said.

"Well, I don't want him. Didn't anyone ever tell him about soap and water, to say nothing of a comb? I bet I can tell you what that slob had for breakfast because it's probably lodged in his beard."

"Now lass, ye have no choice. Ye were promised on yer naming day. Ye belong to this man. It is a woman's lot in life. Make the best of it. He may not be as handsome as Robert, but sex with a wild highlander could prove to be more of a pleasure than a chore." Anna winked knowingly. "I wasn't always old and dried out. My first husband was a highlander. We enjoyed each other every night until he was killed. I would not change that year for anything on earth. My only regret is that I was barren."

Davida thought of Anna's description of Charles as a wild highlander. She'd always fantasized about those men, but she hadn't expected him to look like one of the pillagers in the Capital One commercials.

Chapter Two

Davida allowed her Uncle John to help her get into the wagon driven by a man with worse personal hygiene than Charles—and that was no easy fete.

She cried when they pulled away from the manor house where Davida had spent her childhood. It wasn't because she felt anything for the people who were wishing her well, but because she was afraid of what the future held. If she could get her hands on the little twit who now inhabited her body, enjoyed her central heat, and marveled at her microwave oven, she'd gladly ring her neck.

As they drove across the countryside, she realized a ride in an open wagon across the hills and valleys of Scotland left a lot to be desired. She would have given anything for a pothole-infested country road. It would have been ten times better than this. It was evident these people had never heard of shocks or even springs for the seat.

Beneath her ass, the wooden plank upon which she sat felt like she was on a piece of concrete. To keep her mind off her discomfort, she had kept her eye on the sky and watched as the sun dipped lower in the west. *Don't these idiots know that we should be looking for a place to stop for the night?*

"When will we be stopping?" she asked the grotesque man who sat next to her. "I need to relieve myself."

The man who identified himself as Ian turned to her to reply. "We got at least another hour of daylight. We'll stop then."

His foul breath made her want to retch. She was sorry she'd even asked the question.

The sun sank lower and lower until the troll who sat beside her brought the wagon to a halt at last. Charles rode up to her, dismounted, and helped her down from the seat that seemed to be way too high for her to manage herself.

"How much further is it to the inn?" she asked, once he sat her feet on the ground.

"Inn?" Charles questioned in response. "There is no inn. This is where we will spend the night.

"Here?" she shrieked. "Where will we sleep?" Visions of consummating her marriage with this red-headed Attila the Hun in front of his men assaulted her overactive imagination.

"You will sleep in the wagon while my men and I sleep by the fire."

"In the wagon?"

"Your belongings will be moved and we will give you a fur for your comfort.'"

Supper consisted of hard cheese and stale bread washed down with what Davida could only call piss-warm beer that tasted as bad as it smelled. When they finished eating, the men settled down for the night with not one of them offering to help her move anything.

In the darkness, she tugged on the trunks until she broke most of her fingernails. Finally, she cleared a space just large enough to lie down in the bed of the wagon.

"I didn't like camping when I was a Girl Scout and we had tents and cots," she muttered to herself. The only answer she received was the snores of the men by the fire. *Maybe they all have sleep apnea and they'll die in their sleep. Of course, I couldn't get that lucky.*

By the time morning came, Davida knew every bone in her body ached. The thought of bouncing across the countryside with the troll was even less appealing than it had been the day before.

Since the men were off pissing and shitting in the woods, she crawled out of the wagon by herself and found a bush that afforded her some semblance of privacy. She wanted to bathe, but with no stream nearby she had no choice but to become as gamy as the men with whom she was traveling.

"Where have you been?" Charles demanded when she returned to the makeshift camp.

"Doing the same thing you were doing."

9

"You should have waited for me. You are my wife."

"If I had waited until you decided it was time to come and escort me, I would have wet my…" she floundered for the proper way to say she would have pissed her pants.

"That is my fault," Charles said, his voice softer than she'd heard it before. "It will take me awhile to get used to having someone other than myself to consider."

Davida realized that in whatever time period she'd been dropped, women were little more than property.

* * * *

It was late afternoon and still Charles had not arrived. Gwain was beginning to become worried. One of his brother's men had come to the manor house early in the morning with word that he would arrive with his new bride before nightfall.

In anticipation, he had instructed the servants to prepare a grand meal and to take the tub to the room that had been made up for Davida.

Gwain was apprehensive about this plan his brother had devised. The one thing he never expected was that while Charles was fighting for Scotland he would be injured, rendering him unable to be with a woman. By the same token, he had realized that he desired the company of men.

When he returned home, he had brought his comrade-in-arms as well as his companion, with him. People had accepted Brian who, for all intents and purposes, had his own quarters in the wing of the manor house that Charles occupied. Davida's room would be in that wing of the house as well.

He worried about how the girl would react to being a wife to Charles in name only. He also worried about being the one to father the next heir to the McGowen clan. Could he convince her that this was a secret that must be kept at all costs? From what Charles had said, she was a very sheltered young woman. Would she shy away from such an arrangement?

"Charles is coming, Charles is coming!" a young boy shouted as he ran into the great hall.

All around him people stopped what they were doing to listen to what the boy was saying. Gwain knew the lad would be watching for the arrival of the McGowen men, as his father had left with Charles a fortnight earlier.

Gwain knew that Brian would be attending to the drawing of a hot bath for Charles. Since Brian was none too fond of the idea of Charles returning with a wife, he knew the young man would not make any arrangements for Davida's bath. It was up to him to instruct the servants to begin filling the tub in Davida's chambers with hot water, so that she could wash the dust from the road off her body.

He had no more than given the order when Charles burst into the great hall. "Fill my tub. I am dusty and dirty and I smell. As soon as I am clean, I am looking forward to a hot meal." With that said, he pulled Gwain into a bear hug.

Gwain had to admit he felt relief at having his older brother home. Although the rest of the clan respected him, he was but the younger brother in their eyes and not their leader. During his brother's absence he had given orders, but they had always been questioned. It would not be so with Charles home.

Once Charles released him, Gwain saw the woman who would become his lover. She was indeed young, perhaps not more than twenty winters old. Her red hair was long and thick and her eyes were as green as springtime grass.

"Davida," Charles said, holding out his hand to her. "This is my brother, Gwain."

The look on her face was one of shock. He couldn't help but equate her to a doe caught between two hunters. She seemed tentative about holding out her hand to him. He couldn't decide if she acted in such a way because she was ashamed of her appearance, or if she feared him.

"It is a pleasure to meet the delightful Davida," he said, as he brought her dusty hand to his lips. "The servants have your rooms prepared and I have requested that a hot bath be drawn for you. Once you are bathed and rested, a feast has been prepared in honor of your arrival."

"I trust you will see to Davida's needs, Gwain," Charles said.

Gwain had no doubt about the meaning of his brother's words. By helping Davida with her bath, he would be paving the way for her to become his lover.

"Send Brian to my room to assist me as well," Charles requested.

"He is already there, overseeing the filling of your tub. Between the two of us, we have kept the servants more than busy this day."

* * * *

The young man who stood before her stunned Davida. Suddenly it all made sense. It was no wonder she'd been sent to this time. The year had to be somewhere around 1470, and Gwain was the spirit that had invaded her Ouija board.

Since she was his brother's wife, it was evident that she would soon become his lover, and what a lover he would be. He was well-groomed. Even his beard was neatly trimmed and his hair was clean and freshly cut.

When he pressed her travel-dusty hand to his lips, she knew the real Davida would choose Gwain over Charles. No matter what it cost her, she would make the most of this affair.

It was entirely possible that the twenty-something twit would have a problem with the handsome hunk who tempted her to break her wedding vows, but she wouldn't. While Davida dealt with Denise's hot flashes, dry pussy, and mood swings, Denise who was now Davida, would have the time of her life.

There was something to be said for the wisdom of age and the knowledge she'd gleaned from all those erotic books she'd read since Fred's death. She'd been given a second chance for the sex life she'd been denied the first time around. *This time will be different,* she silently vowed.

When Gwain kissed her hand, it sent a tingle through her body that told her this man could definitely be dangerous. She followed him up to the bedchamber that he indicated would be hers.

"Won't I be sharing a bedroom with Charles?" she asked when he held open the door to an enormous room with a big bed and a fireplace.

"Charles prefers his own bedchamber," Gwain replied. "I, on the other hand, enjoy having a woman in my bed."

The undertone of his meaning was not lost on her. She understood him completely. He intended to have her in his bed, perhaps as soon as Charles did the dirty deed of consummating their marriage.

She ran her tongue over her lips, all the while knowing she was driving him crazy. "Charles frightens me," she confessed as she put her hand to his cheek. She had worked hard to make her voice sound like a frightened child to heighten his curiosity about her.

"There is nothing for you to fear. Allow me to help you prepare for your bath. Once you are warmed and clean, you will feel differently."

You bet I will, buster. I'm dying to see what's beneath your kilt. If I'm lucky, you'll take the damn thing off and join me in the tub. It certainly looks big enough for the two of us.

Before she could put voice to her thoughts, Gwain had closed the door behind them and was helping her out of her clothing.

"What are you doing?" she asked, acting shocked at his actions. In truth, she was completely aroused by him undressing her.

"Only what Charles wants me to do," he replied. He continued unbuttoning the bodice of her blouse. Once he slipped the garment from her shoulders, he untied her undergarment. The feel of the cool air against her breasts being confined since the morning of her wedding was nothing compared to his strong hands caressing her nipples, sending shock waves of desire to her toes.

"Ohhhhhhhh…"she gasped.

"They are beautiful," Gwain commented, his voice soft and sensual. "Ours is going to be a delightful relationship."

At this moment, she didn't care that she was technically a married woman and this was her brother-in-law. It had been so long since a man had loved her, and she wanted him to take her while her body burned with desire.

Rather than continue to turn her on with his touches and kisses, he removed her skirt and undergarments. "Your bath awaits, my lady," he said, taking her hand in his and leading her toward the waiting tub.

She glanced at the tub and then to Gwain. "Will you join me, kind sir?"

"I see no reason not to. The tub is large enough for two and I would enjoy joining you. Once I do, I pray that you will allow me to wash your back."

And my front and my pussy and anything else you want to wash.

Rather than respond verbally, she nodded her head in the hope of perpetuating the myth that she was nothing more than a young maiden.

He proceeded to take off his shirt, revealing a chest that resembled that of the bodybuilders she'd seen on TV, with a sprinkling of red hair accenting his highly sculptured pecks. The hair dwindled to a tantalizing line that trailed down to his kilt. Her hands itched to snatch off the length of plaid that hid his male attributes. Instead, she continued to play the part of demure maiden who merely watched as he disrobed.

She gasped with pleasure when his cock was fully revealed. He was indeed a young, virile man. She couldn't help but notice the shaft that stood at attention, rising from its nest of red hair that hid his jewels within its curls.

Once she was in the tub, he slid in behind her, his cock butting up against her ass until she wanted nothing more than to sigh in delight and enjoy his attentions.

After working up a rich lather on the soft cloth, he reached around her and washed her entire body, paying particular attention to her woman's soul hidden in the moist valley of her woman's cleft. The manipulations of his soap-slick fingers brought her to the brink of orgasm. She shuddered against him and prayed he would never stop. To her disappointment, he removed his hand and began to scrub her back.

"Are you a virgin?" he asked.

In which life? If I can believe the dream I had, Davida is definitely not a virgin, but what if it was only a dream? "Ah...I don't think so."

"You don't sound very certain. It makes no difference. We will know for certain tonight. If you are not, there are ways to fool my brother. For now, we must finish your bath, for the evening meal has been prepared and all of the clan are anxious to see you for the first time."

Reluctantly, Davida allowed Gwain to help her get out of the tub. He stood before her, unashamed of his nakedness. As though he were a bath attendant, he dried her body before helping her to dress.

She was surprised to realize that the clothing he had laid out for her fit perfectly. The plaid he gave her was not the Brice plaid she'd worn since the day of her wedding, but that of the McGowen clan. The color suited her well, and even though she wanted nothing to do with Charles or his clan, she knew she would wear it proudly.

* * * *

Gwain led Davida into the great hall. The high table was set to accommodate four people. It was obvious that Charles and his friend Brian were expected to occupy the two chairs on the left end of the table, while the other two places were left open for him and Davida. If anyone thought that the arrangement was strange, no one mentioned it.

Gwain watched as Davida took a moment to study Charles' appearance. He couldn't fault her for the thoughts that were surely running rampant through her mind. Charles was certainly more handsome than he had appeared before. He not only cut his hair, but he had also trimmed his beard, something that he evidently had not done for many months prior to showing up to claim Davida as his wife. His clean-cut look was enhanced by the fact that Brian was obviously giving him pleasure beneath the table while he made conversation with those around him.

"Is that Charles?" Davida questioned, her mouth agape at the sight of the man who had claimed her as wife.

"Yes. He is a handsome man when he is well-groomed. It was his vow not to cut his hair or beard until he found you. You were promised to him on your naming day. When he returned to your father's keep to claim you sixteen years later, David Brice was dead, and no one knew where you were. It has taken him these four years to find you."

Davida looked at Charles, leaving Gwain to read her thoughts. Would she find her husband more appealing than the younger brother who would bed her as soon as the meal was finished? Gwain hoped not, but had he not always stood in the shadow of his older brother?

He stepped in front of her and held out his hand to help her step up to the high table. Once she was seated, Charles acknowledged her with a nod of his head before he returned his attention to Brian.

"It seems as though my husband is preoccupied," she said as she put her hand on Gwain's knee. With the confidence of a practiced prostitute, she slid it up until she was able to wrap her fingers around his cock. The act made him wonder if she was right about not being a virgin and if she was, why she seemed so apprehensive about the fact.

A growing heat made him wish that the dreaded supper was ended so that he could take her back to her bedchamber and have his way with the saucy wench that she appeared to be. If his brother was feeling half this good with Brian's attention, it was no wonder he was smiling like a besotted fool.

* * * *

Davida stared at Charles in disbelief. With his beard neatly trimmed, his hair cut, and his body cleansed, he was every bit as handsome as Gwain. It was a shame this guy was gay. She could easily have fantasies about a threesome involving Charles and Gwain.

Brian was another story. The man gave her the creeps. He was so openly gay that he fit the outdated stereotype to a tee. It was evident that these people saw nothing strange about Brian and Charles' relationship, so who was she to say anything? In the twenty-first century she'd learned to accept such relationships. She knew she could do no less considering her position.

Ahead of her, Gwain stood on the raised dais, his hand outstretched toward her. Without hesitation, she held out her own hand in response, and allowed him to help her up onto the platform that stood several inches above the floor and elevated them above the rest of the clan. As though oblivious to her state of mind, Gwain held out her chair, inviting her to take the seat next to Charles. Even though she would have been more comfortable further away from her husband, she graciously took the seat that was offered.

Out of courtesy she turned to acknowledge her husband, only to be snubbed by his curt response before he returned his attention to Brian. Not to be out-snubbed, she waited until Gwain sat down next to her. When he did, she slipped her hand under his kilt. She smiled when her fingers found first his knee and then moved higher until they not only touched, but also curled around his cock. It pleased her to find it was as thick as the trunk of the young maple tree in the front yard of her twenty-first century home.

This certainly beats anything Fred ever had. She could hardly believe the wicked thought that had just crossed her mind.

Beside her, Charles got to his feet. She wondered how he had managed to persuade Brian to loosen his grip, for it was evident that Brian was doing the same thing to Charles that she was doing to Gwain.

16

"As you can all see," he declared, his voice echoing off the walls of the manor house, "my quest has ended. I have found the beautiful Davida, who was promised to me on her naming day. We were married at her uncle's keep, but by mutual consent have decided not to consummate our union until we return home."

Davida knew her eyes opened wide with shock. *No one told me of this decision. This guy is a real fruitcake in more ways than one.*

"Tonight we ask you to celebrate with us," he continued as he held out his hand to help her to her feet.

Reluctantly, she let go of the part of Gwain's body that she know would give her great pleasure. She forced a smile as Charles' large hand circled her smaller one. Although his hand was calloused, his touch was not unpleasant. If he weren't gay, he would have been the one to become her lover once the festivities were concluded. The thought was one that set her mind to spinning. *What if this guy is really bisexual? If so, what if he wants a foursome. This could prove to be quite interesting.*

Chapter Three

Davida waited in her bedchamber. Would it be Gwain or Charles who came to fulfill the husbandly duty of consummating this marriage?

She turned to stare into the full-length freestanding mirror. The woman who stared back at her was a stranger. *Does the real Davida wonder how she has become Denise? Do the mature breasts, paunchy belly, and gray hair look as alien to her as this body does to me?*

"Are you pondering the problems of the world?"

She looked beyond her reflection to the man who stood behind her and was also reflected in the mirror. Her green eyes locked onto Gwain's hazel eyes as they sparkled in the glass before her. She couldn't help but wonder why Charles had been so adamant about their marriage when he was definitely gay and had sent his brother to do the one thing that should have been his by right or marriage.

"I was but thinking of what will happen tonight and why it is you in my bed and not Charles."

"You know the answer to at least one of your questions, if not both. What is a mystery to me is why you are not kicking and screaming because of what Charles did to your lover?"

How can I answer him? Will he believe that he called me to this lifetime through the Ouija board? Or did Davida somehow arrange this through the soothsayer that I was told she had consulted?

"I hardly knew Robert," she said, hoping the white lie wouldn't come back to bite her in the ass. "I would have been marrying a stranger, so it doesn't matter which stranger is the one who claims me as his wife."

18

From my dream, it does matter. Robert was a little boy compared to this guy. I mean, I thought he had a great package from what my dream revealed, but he can't hold a candle to Gwain.

"Someday you will tell me the truth, but for now, I have other things on my mind."

He slipped his hand into the recesses of the bodice of her sleeping gown. As he caressed her breasts, he aroused her until her nipples hardened and she became so wet she wanted him right now. Of course, that was the fifty-something mind of Denise working overtime. Twenty-something Davida wouldn't be so eager, or would she?

"Oh Gwain, don't tease me."

"Teasing isn't want I had in mind," he said, as he swept her into his arms and carried her to the bed. Before he lowered her far enough so that she could touch the bed, he raised her gown over her bare buttock. Brazenly, he caressed the tender flesh of her backside before slipping his fingers across her asshole and into the backside of the moist valley that hid not only her channel of pleasure, but also the heart of her woman's soul. The very act made her ache to touch his ass and play with his balls.

"Put me down," she gasped, her voice breathless with the desire that he had brought to the forefront of her mind. "Let me give you pleasure."

"Not tonight, my love. I'm certain you think you know what transpires between a man and a woman, but I doubt it. You are young and perhaps have mistaken love play for lovemaking."

Look Buster, I know the difference between foreplay and intercourse. I just don't know how far this chick went with Robert.

She made no verbal response to his comment. Instead, she became lost in the ecstasy of his manipulations to her body. This man was, indeed, a practiced lover. His touch was gentle, as though he was used to coaxing virgins to complete arousal.

"There will be pain," he explained, as he lowered her to the bed and positioned himself over her to complete the act to turn her from girl to woman.

Like, duh, this guy is going to be surprised where there is no pain, just expected pleasure. I wonder how he's going to fake the fact that I don't shed virgin's blood?

His cock teased her pussy lips until it found entrance to the channel that she knew would give her pleasure she hadn't enjoyed in years.

To her surprise, she felt as though Gwain was treading into virgin territory. As he pushed harder, she felt the tearing of the fragile membrane that separated virginity from full womanhood. The shock of what was happening to her brought a shriek of surprise from her lips.

When Gwain broke through her final barrier, he stopped his movements to allow her to adjust to the size of him within her body.

Well, I'll be damned. This chick was a virgin. I haven't felt like this since Fred popped my cherry in the backseat of his '57 Chevy.

Before her mental ramblings were completed, Gwain began to move, filling her body with pleasure she thought she would never again experience in her lifetime. She was delighted to find that the lubrication of Davida's young body far exceeded that provided by the KY jelly she and Fred had used since she started menopause.

"Your body tells me two things," he whispered when he paused in his movements to prolong the pleasure they were both experiencing.

"What are you trying to tell me?" she inquired.

"As I thought, you were a virgin, but your body tells me you have the body of a woman in lust. Never before have I had a virgin so versed in the art of lovemaking. Perhaps someday you will enlighten me as to how a virgin can so easily take on the role of a practiced lover."

Honey, you'd never believe me if I told you the truth. Just continue what you're doing. The other thing can wait.

She wanted to tell him that she hadn't felt like this for over thirty years. She'd been just sixteen the first time Fred made love to her. The act had awakened her sexuality. Every month she prayed she wasn't pregnant and had been relieved when her period came on schedule. It wasn't until they were married and wanted a child that they learned she couldn't have children. Back then there had been none of the procedures that childless couples engaged in during the twenty-first century. Their only option had been adoption, and their financial situation had been a drawback that kept them childless.

"Davida."

The sound of Gwain saying her name melted the memories of Fred and the reality of her life in the twenty-first century.

"Is something wrong?" he asked before she had a chance to speak.

"Nothing is wrong. I-I was just thinking of the children you and I could…" An onslaught of tears cut short her words.

"The thought of children should not bring tears to your eyes. There must be something more than you are telling me."

To her regret, he withdrew and rolled to his side to take her into his arms in comfort. "Why are you stopping?" she asked, bewildered by his actions.

"You are upset. Something bothers you about making love with me. Will you tell me what it is?"

Davida took a deep breath. How could she tell him that she'd been summoned by his spirit on the Ouija board, or worse yet, transported by some well-meaning soothsayer who listened to a frightened young woman? "I-I don't know where to begin. I don't know if you'll understand."

He put his finger under her chin, turned, and lifted her face until their eyes met. "You can tell me anything. I realize this is a strange situation."

Before she could reply, he captured her lips and kissed her tenderly, while manipulating her right breast with his large hand. The pleasure he gave her drove away all thoughts of the frustrated tears she had shed over her lifetime for the babies who were never conceived.

"Now," he said, once he released her lips, "what is it that makes you so sad?"

"It's a long story and…"

The door to the bedchamber suddenly opened. From instinct rather than embarrassment, Davida pulled the blanket up to cover her nakedness.

"Have you shed virgin's blood?" Charles demanded.

"What do you care?" Davida questioned. "You have sent…"

"Be quiet, woman. I speak to my brother, your lover."

"I will not be quiet. It should be you in my bed and not Gwain. You are my husband."

Gwain put his hand on her arm in an attempt to silence her. "She does not understand, Charles. She did shed virgin's blood. The rest I will explain to her. Now leave us alone."

As though he was a chastised child, Charles backed out of the room, closing the door behind him.

"You must be careful what you say to Charles," Gwain warned. "His temper runs hot, especially about why he searched so diligently to find you to be his wife."

Davida propped herself up on one elbow so she could look Gwain in the eye. As she did, the blanket slipped down, revealing her breasts to his scrutiny.

"Then help me to understand. Why is my virginity so important?"

"I'd rather make love to you. Explanations are for the light of day. The night is meant for love."

"Look Buster, this night had better be meant for telling me what I want to know, or this bedchamber will be very cold and it won't be because of a draft coming through the cracks in the windows."

"What manner of speech is it that comes from your mouth?" he asked, the tone of his voice denoting shock at her use of the slang that would not have been improper if she'd been Denise.

Davida put her hand to her mouth, shocked at the twenty-first century verbiage that had slipped passed her lips.

"It is something I heard from a traveler in my uncle's home. Life has not been easy since the death of my father." She knew he didn't quite believe her, but at least he didn't press her to explain further. She realized to do so with him would not be acceptable.

She allowed him to take her in his arms and press his hard cock against what she now knew was her virginal cunt. Love juices surged from inside her body to bring more natural lubrication to her hidden channel of pleasure. Explanations from both of them could wait until morning. For now, her body screamed for sexual satisfaction.

* * * *

Davida's outspoken attitude bothered Gwain, but not enough to deny the hunger of his cock for her nether-regions. With her being a virgin, he did not want to move too quickly. Instead, he planned to savor the experience.

Even though he needed no coaxing to regain his erection, he knew from experience that a woman's body needed more stimulation to be ready for sexual activity. He turned to face her and took one of her perfect breasts into his hand. They were not the mature breasts of the women from the village that sagged from years of childbearing and age. Neither were they small like the young maidens in the village. Davida's breasts were firm and full. They filled his large hands perfectly.

She reached for his cock, but he stopped her. "Tonight is for me to pleasure you. Did I not tell you this earlier?"

"You did," she agreed, "but it does not seem fair. Why should I receive all the pleasure and you get nothing in return?"

He couldn't help but smile at her ignorance. His pleasure had been heightened by the fact that he was the first man to enter her body, and had increased with each thrust he made within the warm velvety folds of the part of her that had been made to be filled with no one but him. "We will have much time for such things, as soon winter will be upon us. When the snow is deep. We will have many long days when you will be free to do whatever you wish with my body."

He was pleased when she relaxed and opened herself to him. He moved into a more comfortable position. Then he leaned over the upper part of her body to kiss one of the globes of her breasts. He trained his kisses down until his lips caressed her nipple. He teased the hard nub with first his tongue and then his teeth. The sound of her contented moans and mews told him that she enjoyed the attention he was paying to her glorious breasts.

While he worshipped her hardened nipple with his mouth, he moved his hand to the mound of tangled curls that hid her woman's delights from his sight. As much as he wanted to entangle his fingers in those curls, he pressed further until he touched the moist crevice that housed the nub of her clit. Using a circular motion, he rubbed it until her moans became screams of pleasure and love juices flowed from her body.

"Please Gwain, take me now. I can't stand this passionate torture any longer."

He released her breast and positioned himself over her. "There will be no pain this time," he promised as he slid his cock deep within her cunt. With no resistance from her virgin's barrier, he cock plunged in and out until the pleasure of it brought him to the point of no return. He had no choice but to spill his seed, even though he wanted to prolong the pleasure longer.

23

He felt her climax at the same time as he did. Of the many women he had loved in the past, none of them had reacted in quite this way before. This woman was meant to be his, even though she was bound as wife to his brother.

As was his practice, he went to the hearth to take some warm water from the container, and then sat next to the fire to be warmed. After putting it in a small bowl, he picked up the linen clothes he had ordered to be laid out for this purpose earlier in the evening.

Davida was almost asleep when he returned to the bed to cleanse her nether-lips and legs of the love juices that lingered there. When he touched her with the wet cloth, she immediately opened her eyes.

"What are you doing?"

"I am cleansing you so that when you awaken you will be fresh. When I was a young man, I was fostered to a man who was a great lover. He taught me the many ways a man can pleasure a woman. The cleansing is but one of the things he felt was pleasing to a woman."

She relaxed as he savored the sight of her pussy. It was wet with their combined juices and her clit was swollen from the passion they had just enjoyed.

Although he hardened at the thought of sucking her in that special place, he did nothing to relieve the ache in his cock. There would be many nights for him to show her the skills he had learned from his mentor.

Chapter Four

Davida awoke and turned to where Gwain had been when she fell asleep. Instead of the man who had given her such pleasure only hours earlier, she saw only the empty space where he had slept. The pillow still carried the scent of his hair. The essence of him that lingered brought back memories of the night of passion they had shared.

She knew she should get out of bed and clean up before dressing for the day, but instead she snuggled down under the covers. In this time period, there was no need for her to get up. Charles was the head of his clan and as his wife there would be little for her to do. With no computer, she had no need to check for e-mail or play senseless card games, therefore, no real reason to hurry getting out of bed.

She had just fallen back to sleep when there was a knock on the door. She knew it wasn't Charles, for he wouldn't bother to knock. "Come in," she called, as she pulled the coverlet up around her neck.

To her surprise, a young woman who carried a strong resemblance to both Gwain and Charles entered the room. "Good morning, Davida. I am Charles' and Gwain's sister, Briana. Gwain asked me to come to help you dress."

"But…but I thought…"

"I know you thought Gwain would be here, but he has duties to attend to. He asked me to help you and to try and explain this whole mess."

Davida threw aside the covers and shivered at the chill of the room as she got out of bed. There was no need to hide her nakedness from her sister-in-law. As soon as the covers were thrown back, Briana checked

25

the bed linens for the bloodstain that would, indeed, prove Davida's virginity.

"It is a strange situation you have found yourself in, lass, strange indeed. Even though Charles and Gwain think they are being discreet, it is no secret among the clan who will father their next leader. Only their fear of Charles' wrath keeps them from saying anything about it."

"Other than the obvious reason, why was it Gwain in my bed last night? I know that even men like Charles are capable of fathering children. Why was it so important for him to marry me if he did not want me? Why did he feel he had to kill the man I was to marry before he took me away from everything I have known for the past several years?"

The questions sounded silly even to Davida. She had known none of what had been taken from her, not really, but the real Davida had. It was the same with Robert. He had been the one the real Davida longed to marry, but to her he was little more than another stranger who had so dramatically entered her life.

"It is a long story. I will tell it to you while I help you with your morning preparations."

Davida watched as Briana dipped warm water from the container by the fireplace and brought it along with soap and towels to the table where she had indicated that Davida should sit. While Davida cleansed her hands and face, Briana continued.

"Charles is the oldest and when the clan was called upon to fight the English, it was his duty to go. Unfortunately, there are not enough whores to take care of the needs of so many. In those cases, men like Brian take care of the needs of their fellow soldiers. At first it was hard for Charles to accept this, but Brian made things much easier because of his persuasion when it comes to relations. To him, women are not attractive, but men are."

Davida knew she should have been shocked, but she'd read enough historical stories to know such things happened. What came as a surprise was how easily Briana spoke of such things.

"So Charles learned that he also liked men better than women?"

Briana laughed at Davida's question. "You are perceptive. He does enjoy being with Brian, but that is not the reason he sent for Gwain. Charles was badly injured in the fighting. The physician that attended to him said he would never be able to love a woman and give her the pleasure she deserved, nor would he be able to father children. That is something that was never to be known by the clan, but you know how gossip spreads within families. If the child Charles calls his son belongs to Gwain, no one other than the clan will ever know."

Davida knew all about gossip and families. It had run rampant when she and Fred couldn't have children. As everything that Briana said started to fall into place, Davida began to see the bigger picture. There was no way Charles could have romanced a woman, knowing that he could not ask her to be his wife. By turning to the woman who had been promised to him on her naming day, he wouldn't have to prove anything to her before marriage.

As she had personally seen, he had taken Davida far from her family and home to force her into the arms of his brother. Being so far from family, there would be no one for her to talk to about the strange relationship between the two brothers and the woman one called "wife" and the other called "mistress."

* * * *

Gwain returned from the stables where he assessed the new stallion his brother had brought with him as a gift for being a physical husband to Davida. The days he knew would be long, but they would be tolerated because the nights promised delightful lovemaking.

The thought of Davida brought to mind the things they had promised to tell each other by the light of day. He had not been able to tell her the reason he was the man in her bed. He prayed Briana would be able to make Davida understand about the relationship between Charles, Davida, and himself.

He'd eaten early so he could be away from the house when Charles and Davida came down to eat the morning meal with the clan, who were there to celebrate the consummation of Charles' marriage.

When Charles had summoned him back to the manor house, he had been honor-bound to return. He certainly never expected to find a woman like Davida who would be able to make him fall hopelessly in love.

It was hard to believe that he even belonged to this clan. He had been but a youth of six winters when his father fostered him out to his mother's brother. While Charles learned the art of war from their father, Gwain learned to read, to cipher, and to love. Although they were brothers by blood, they were different in every other aspect.

"Are ye not eating with the clan, laddie?"

Gwain looked up to see his father's brother, Angus, standing in the doorway of the stable. "This is Charles' day. You know I don't belong here. I have come and continue to stay at Charles' request. At first it was to oversee the clan while he searched for Davida, now it is to share his joy. At his request, I will remain until the naming day of his first son."

"Ye do not fool me, laddie. I have known ye both since the day ye were born. As your father's younger brother, I know all that transpires in this family. Your father confided in me as to the extent of Charles' injuries. It is not common knowledge, but ye can always talk to me. Take care that you do not fall in love with the lass. You must know that forever and for always she is your brother's wife."

"Thank you, Uncle Angus. I feel that my position in Charles' household is close to that between you and my father."

"That it is, lad, but never did your father ask such a thing of me. I was the one to tell your father to foster you out. Being the younger brother in a clan like this does not bode well. I should know, for I have lived in the shadow of my older brother all of my life. Do not become Charles' pawn, as I did for your father."

Angus clasped Gwain's hand before turning to return to the house and the announcement that Charles would make about Davida's virginity. He would brag about what a great lover he was, and how he knew that he and Davida would become parents of the next heir to the leadership of the clan.

The words that Angus spoke about not falling in love with Davida were too close to reality for Gwain. He had been with many women before, but never one who had a cunt that so perfectly fit his cock.

When she had professed to be uncertain of her virginity, he had been confused. His plan had been to cut his finger to produce the virgin's blood that Charles desired. The fact that she was in reality a virgin, and yet questioned that virginity, was a puzzlement. The uncle who had fostered him would say she was like an onion. Once you peeled away the

28

outer layer and thought you knew her, there was another layer waiting to be uncovered.

Footsteps of someone entering the stable ended his mental ramblings. He turned to see Brian standing behind him.

"Was the bitch really a virgin or did you tell Charles only what he wanted to hear?"

"Why should you care?"

"Because what affects Charles affects me as well. I love him. If she was not a virgin when you took her, it could be possible that she carries another man's bastard."

"Trust me, she was a virgin."

"Then you didn't fake the virgin's blood that Charles is so intent on bragging about?"

"It was what I had planned to do to save her from Charles' wrath, but it was not necessary." He held out his hands so that Brian could see that none of his fingers carried a mark from where he would have cut himself to produce the required blood.

"I do not like any of this," Brian declared. "Why could things not have gone on as they have since I first met Charles?"

Gwain felt pity for the man. He was the kind of soldier who was not abhorred when asked to satisfy the sexual needs of his comrades. When Charles had been injured and rendered incapable of being sexually active with a woman, Brian had not deserted him.

What the two of them did in the privacy of Charles' bedchamber was of no concern to him. Unfortunately, once Gwain went back to his uncle's estate, Davida would be concerned by it. In no way could he imagine her being content to live a life without the physical love of a man. He would have to talk to Charles about arranging for a lover for his wife. Considering the way she had responded to his lovemaking even before they were in the wedding bed, and especially as she learned more about bed sport, she would be even more devastated living a celibate life. Just thinking of the time he spent in the tub as well as the bed with her made his cock swell with desire.

"I doubt your life will change, Brian. You will still have Charles all to yourself at night. Davida is the one who will suffer. As soon as her son is delivered and named, I will be gone and she will spend the rest of her life alone."

Brian looked at him in disbelief. The only words to pass his lips were profanities. With no further civil conversation, he took his horse from the stable.

Gwain watched Brian saddle his horse and took note of which direction he had ridden. He wanted no further contact with the man this morning. He would make certain that when he rode out, it would be in the opposite direction to assure his solitude.

* * * *

Davida allowed Briana to help her dress for the day. She was still reeling from the things her sister-in-law had told her and was trying to put it all in perspective. She now realized it was time to perpetuate the lie that Charles had taken her virginity hours earlier.

Charles waited for her at the entrance to the great hall. She couldn't help but be amazed by the difference in his appearance from when he had invaded her uncle's home and claimed her as his bride. With his hair cut, his beard trimmed, and the grime of travel washed from his body, he was very handsome. If circumstances were different, she knew she could have been satisfied with him in her bed.

As soon as the thought crossed her mind, she remembered the night of delightful pleasures she's shared with Gwain. In all of her married life with Fred, she had never experienced an orgasm during sex. The only times she had come close to anything like what she experienced last night came when she would masturbate while Fred snored.

"Good morning, my dear," Charles greeted her. He took her hand and led her to the high table. "I trust you slept well after our night of pleasure."

She knew this was what the clan had gathered to hear, but the lie burned like acid on her tongue. "Yes," she replied, her voice hardly more than a whisper. "I slept very well, thank you."

"But did she shed virgin's blood?" someone called out.

The question brought back the memory of the pain associated with Gwain breaking the barrier between girl and woman. Just the memory brought a smile to her lips, as the pain associated with the loss of virginity had been immediately replaced by the extreme pleasure that followed.

"Your question brings a smile to the lips of my bride. I swear that until our night of love, her virginity was intact. If you do not believe me, ask Briana, for she checked the bedding while she helped Davida dress for the day."

A cheer went up from those gathered in the hall. It was evident that Charles more than appreciated the acceptance of the clan and reveled in their celebration. After what seemed like an eternity, Charles held up his hand for silence.

"Soon Davida and I will be announcing the expected birth of our first child. From one night together, I can tell you that ours will be an exciting match."

His statement made Davida wonder just how much Charles knew about her night of pleasure with Gwain.

"Did you think my brother didn't tell me what you were like in bed?" Charles whispered in her ear.

The words made her uneasy but not the feel of his breath against her ear and then her neck. If things were different, he would be her husband in every way and she had no doubt he could have fulfilled his husbandly duties.

When he began to nibble on her ear, she squirmed with the desire she knew the man at her side could not quench. She looked around the room and realized that Gwain was not seated with the rest of the clan. After last night, how could he not be there to see the desire in her eyes?

Even without asking the question aloud, she knew the answer. It was Charles' belief that only a handful of people knew that her child would belong to Gwain. After Briana's warning, it was best if she not allow him to think otherwise. From what she gathered, the man had a temper and it was best if she not provoke it in any way.

In order to keep the myth of her happiness with her husband alive, she turned her attention to him. She prayed her actions would make it look like she was well satisfied with him.

Davida knew her act must have worked because of the smile that graced his full lips when he leaned over to kiss her tenderly. "I have much work to do today, lass, but tonight we will quench the passion that radiates from your eyes."

Everyone in the hall laughed as though they were enjoying the love play that sounded in his voice.

"Yes, Charles, tonight will, indeed, quench my passion."

He pulled her into a warm embrace and kissed her again before their breakfast was served.

She knew, as did he, that tonight she and Gwain would share renewed passion. What neither man knew was that somehow fate had given her a chance at being young and in love. This time there would be no one to chide her for wanting to fulfill her most erotic fantasies, and she planned to make the most of the opportunity. She'd done enough reading to know that she could show Gwain tricks that the man had no idea even existed.

Chapter Five

The day, which had started out with clear blue skies and southerly breezes, turned cold quickly as the wind shifted to the north and storm clouds gathered. Gwain was far out on the moors when the weather changed. By the time he returned to the manor house, the fall sun was slipping beneath the western horizon and the first drops of cold rain were beginning to fall.

As he stabled his horse, he noticed that the mare Brian had ridden earlier had been left in her stall. On closer examination, he saw that the man had not taken the time to remove the saddle from the poor beast's back. It was likely she hadn't been rubbed down properly either. As he had noticed in the past several months, Brian was a lazy bastard who demanded that the servants do the work he should have done himself. After unsaddling his horse and rubbing him down, he turned to do the same for Brian's mount.

Once he finished his tasks in the stable, Gwain headed for the manor house. He was more than ready for a glass of whiskey, the warmth of the hall, and the meal he knew would soon be served.

"Where have ye been, lad?" Angus inquired as soon as he entered the house. "Had ye not returned soon, I was going to go out to search for you myself."

"I rode out into the moors. When the weather changed, I was far from the house. All the way back I thought of some of the clan's good whiskey or perhaps a tankard of ale. I would have been in earlier, but I found that Brian had neglected his horse again. That poor animal deserves much better than that man for her master. I unsaddled her and

33

gave her a good rubdown before I came into the house. If I thought it would do any good, I'd speak to Charles about him, but that is one battle I do not intend to instigate."

"Ye are wise to choose yer battles, Gwain. Perhaps ye should think twice about your other duties as well. If I were in yer boots, I would not be thinkin' of spirits to warm my being when there is a beautiful lass who can do it for ye. Davida was radiant when she broke her fast and Charles declared that her virginity had been taken. It was evident she had been fucked and fucked well. From the look on her face, tonight will be even better, but only if you are not too drunk to enjoy it."

Gwain laughed heartily as he accepted a tankard of ale from his uncle. The liquid warmed its way to his belly. He would be careful not to consume too much of the potent brew in order to bring warmth to his body. Instead he moved closer to the hearth and enjoyed the heat produced by the peat that was stored from the moors as well as the precious logs that added fuel to the fire.

Once he was warmed he took a seat at the back of the hall so he could watch Davida without anyone becoming suspicious about his connection to her. With the chill that hung in the air, she had dressed in a purple wool dress with a length of plaid over her shoulder. The shade of the dress reminded him of the heather that bloomed in the spring as well as the fall.

Before his eyes, Charles took a piece of roasted duckling in his fingers and held it up to Davida's lips. Delicately, she nibbled at the piece of meat, and then licked his fingers. To all who watched, they were a loving and devoted couple. To him, the scene brought on waves of jealousy. *I should be the one feeding her. It should be my fingers she licks in appreciation.*

"Be careful, laddy," Angus warned. "Do not be so concerned with the act they put on for the clan. There are those who do not respect Charles and would take any opportunity to soil his name and remove him as head of the clan."

"Do you not think the thought of doing the same hasn't crossed my mind? He has a temper that is known throughout Scotland and as far away as the courts of London. I understand his anger is because of his condition, but does it not hamper his ability to lead?"

34

"Ye know it does not. As I said before, he has put you in an awkward position. Ye cannot jeopardize your brother's position. Remember what awaits ye at yer uncle's estate."

Gwain lowered his eyes to avoid Angus' gaze. As he did, he realized that with his eyes trained on the plate of food in front of him he would not have to watch Charles and Davida. *Tonight, my love, tonight I will be in your bed. Only by the dark of night will you belong to me.*

"The sight of the two of them together makes me want to retch."

Gwain looked up to see that Brian had joined him at the table. "They are man and wife. They are merely doing what is expected of them."

"It is I who belongs at the high table, not some country bitch that he picked up along the road. The man exasperates me. He brings in strays as though they were treasured pets."

Gwain felt his temper begin to boil. "At least Charles knows how to treat both humans and animals. It was I who had to unsaddle your horse and give her a rubdown. Are you really as stupid as you look, or do you not know how to treat the living creatures that you seem to think are there for your pleasure only?"

"I have never unsaddled a horse, nor have I given one a rubdown. The thought of either task is disgusting. That is the reason one has servants."

"Perhaps there are servants in your father's household, but within the clan each man is expected to pull his own weight, even if he is my brother's lover."

Gwain could see that his words had prompted Brian to an anger that would someday be his undoing. He balled and unballed his fists, and for one moment Gwain wished the man would strike the first blow and give him reason to bloody his face and take the milksop grin from his lips.

"Charles and I will discuss your vile accusations. If you do not watch your step, your position in this household could easily be reversed. It is not only I who lives off the generosity of Charles, but you as well."

Gwain returned his attention to his food. In no way did he want to bring Davida into the conversation that had turned so bitter. Like it or not, Gwain would remain in the household until the naming day of his son. Then he would return to his uncle's estate and claim the birthright promised him. With his uncle having only daughters, his estate and all of

35

his monies were to go to Gwain upon his death. His cousins had married well and each received generous dowries. With those obligations met, the estate and the monies left to Gwain would be more than enough to last him the rest of his life.

* * * *

Davida accepted the roast duck from Charles' fingers and licked the grease from them. Earlier, Charles had instructed her how to act in front of the clan. The deception disgusted her, but she knew it was one in which she had to take part.

Not only had Briana instructed her as to her duties as mistress of the manor, she had also told her of Charles' temper when things did not go his way. In no way did she want to be at the mercy of his fists. With his hands spread on the table where he was feeding her, she could imagine the strength of them when they were balled into lethal weapons.

At the back of the hall, she saw Gwain watching them intently. Just seeing him brought to mind the plans she had for him tonight. From the look in his eyes, she knew Gwain wished he were the one feeding her the roast duckling.

Davida averted her eyes so as not to show her desire for the man who had shared her bed last night. Instead, she purposely turned her attention to Charles. He, in turn, slipped his hand from the table to rest it first on her knee and then to pull on the hem of her skirt in order to run his hand up her leg until he found her pubic hair and then the moist crevice that it hid.

"From the way you are already wet," he whispered in her ear, "it is evident that my brother will have a wild night ahead of him. It is a shame that it has to be Gwain and not me who occupies your bed."

With the words spoken he pinched her clit until it was all she could do not to scream out in pain. The tears that pooled in her eyes seemed to bring delight to Charles.

"Be prepared, for some night I may be tempted to join the two of you in your chamber. It could be interesting to see what you can do to two brothers at the same time."

The thought sickened her. She didn't want to make love to anyone but Gwain, and yet she would have no say in the matter.

As suddenly as Charles had taken liberties with her, he stopped. To her disgust, he licked her essence from his fingers before he looked out across the crowded hall. As soon as he did, he became suddenly preoccupied.

She followed his gaze until she saw Brian taking a seat next to Gwain. Instead of staring, she studied her husband's expression. It was evident that Charles was fond of Brian, perhaps even cared deeply for him, but she did not see the love that radiated from Brian's eyes mirrored in those of her husband. He had settled for something less than love because of his injuries. It was sad to think that such a brave man had settled for less than what he deserved.

"Is something wrong, my dear?" Charles asked, when he caught her looking at him.

"Nothing is wrong. I was only wondering what Brian is thinking about when we are together like this. He has been a loyal and true friend to you. It is not often that one finds a friend of such merit."

Charles took her hand and held it to his lips. "My wife is as wise as she is beautiful. I must say I worried as to how you would adjust to this situation."

"I am your wife. It is my duty to adapt to whatever situation my husband deems proper." The words made her sick to her stomach. *When I married Fred in the sixties, I fought like a she-bear to keep the word "obey" out of our vows. What a hypocrite I've become.*

"What did you do to occupy your day?" Charles asked, as though they were any normal married couple in any period of time.

"Briana gave me a tour of the house. I was very impressed with the kitchen. The meals I have enjoyed here are some of the best I have ever eaten." *Let's face it, the only cooking I do anymore is in the microwave. It's quicker but it certainly doesn't make the food taste this good.*

"I am happy that this house is to your liking. This is to be your home for the remainder of your life. It is where we will raise our children. The servants will be pleased to hear your compliments."

Davida gave him a smile. *Will I ever get used to servants? I can't allow anyone to figure out that I'm not Davida and I know very little of this time period. As for the children, they will belong to Charles in name only. To me, they will always belong to Gwain.*

37

* * * *

With the meal ended, the women retired for the night, allowing the men to enjoy a drop of whiskey and talk over the events of the day.

Gwain tried to concentrate on what was being said around him, but the thought of Davida waiting in her bedchamber dominated his thoughts. By the time Charles retired for the night, Gwain's cock felt as though it would explode. After waiting for an appropriate length of time, he excused himself to go up to bed.

He was pleased that his chamber opened into the one occupied by Davida. With the rest of the clan that occupied the manor house quartered in the other wing of the house, as well as the great room, no one would know where he spent the night.

"I thought you weren't coming," she said, her voice soft as that of a mewing kitten.

A fire burned in the grate, giving off a warm light that complimented the glow from the candles that burned in the room. She sat in the chair next to the fireplace, her naked body glowing as though she wanted it to be the first thing he saw when he entered the room. Bathed in that light, Davida looked like a redheaded angel sent from God for his pleasure.

Her skin glowed with the radiance of youth. To his surprise and pleasure, her nipples had been rubbed with something that turned them an inviting red. A glance around the room showed him a bowl of juicy fall berries sitting on a table next to the hearth where Davida sat to enjoy the warmth of the fire.

"I did not want any of the clan to guess where I spend my nights. It is bad enough that Briana and Uncle Angus know of our secret.

She held out her hand to him and he took it to help her to her feet. "You are so beautiful. Although I would have never wished my brother ill, I am pleased that it is my duty to plant the seed of the next generation to rule the clan."

He pulled her into his arms and kissed her tenderly. He could not believe her brazen actions when she began to remove first his shirt and then his britches. The moment her fingers curled around his cock, it sprang to life as though pleased to be released from the constraints of his clothing.

38

He cupped her breast in his hand and lowered his head in order to suck the sweetness of the juice from her nipple. The taste of the berries combined with the salty essence of Davida's skin to excite him even further.

"Where did you get such a delightful idea?" he asked when he raised his head in order to begin sucking the juice from her second nipple.

She looked up and allowed their eyes to meet. "It is something I read about while in my uncle's household."

Although he didn't believe her story, he said nothing. While he'd been taught to read and write in his uncle's home, he knew that few households taught such things, especially to their daughters. If he weren't secure in the knowledge of her virginity, he would have thought her a woman of the world.

"It matters not where you learned of such erotic pleasures," he finally said. "I will show you more love games tonight."

To his surprise, she put her finger to his lips. "Not tonight. Last night you pleasured me. Tonight it is my turn to do the same for you."

Before he could protest, she took his cock in her hand and led him to the bed where they had shared such pleasures but one night earlier.

At her command, he lay down on his back. Once he did, she knelt between his legs and took his cock in her mouth. Never before had he experienced pleasure of this nature.

While she imitated intercourse using her mouth instead of her cunt, she teased his balls with her fingers. Just when he thought he could stand no more of it, she released his cock, only to begin sucking on his balls.

If he thought the pleasure she'd given him earlier was better than anything he'd ever encountered before, this was beyond compare. "What are you doing to me, woman?"

She stopped and rose up to look at him. "Don't you like this?"

Her voice was deep and husky with desire. From the training he'd received at the hands of his uncle, he knew she was more than ready to be fucked for the rest of the night.

"It is the most intense pleasure I have ever enjoyed. I have been with many women, but have never experienced anything like this before. Where you learned of such things a proper maiden has no way of knowing is beyond me, but I am glad that you know them."

* * * *

Gwain's comment made Davida realize she had made a bad mistake. Telling him she had learned her erotic behavior by reading was the worst thing she could have said. In this time period, proper young ladies were taught to keep a house, handle household servants, and to sew. What they weren't taught was to read. She knew she couldn't take back the words that had slipped past her lips without even realizing it. She also knew that she would have to be more careful in the future. Rather than dwelling on her mistake, she returned to her lovemaking as though she was unaware of her guffaw.

The blowjob she gave to Gwain combined with the sucking of his balls to make her hotter than hell and so wet that Davida knew she would never make it as a seductress. She needed him inside her to ease the ache of desire.

Instead of assuming the missionary position, Davida straddled Gwain's prone body and allowed his stiff cock into her wet pussy. She had always wanted to try different positions with Fred, but he didn't. This was her one and only chance to do all the things she had only read about and yearned to experience.

From this position, the way his cock filled her cunt in places she didn't know existed were touched and brought to life. Even her clit felt differently since his cock rubbed against it seductively with every thrust.

Without realizing it, a shriek of pleasure passed her lips. As her screams echoed off the stone walls of her chamber, her body shuddered in release. The orgasm that held her in the throes of pleasure sent a shudder of delight throughout her entire body.

Why wasn't it like this with Fred? Her mind screamed the question over and over again as she at last relaxed in Gwain's embrace. No answers rushed into her mind, because there were no answers, only those that she already knew. Fred was never obsessed with sex in the same way as her friends' husbands. Making love had been a chore, like taking out the trash and mowing the lawn. The only sex they'd had in years was when she asked him to make love to her, and then it was nothing like this.

"You're purring," Gwain said, as he caressed the curve of her breast.

"Purring?" she questioned.

"You know like a contented kitten. Are you contented in our lovemaking?"

She looked up to stare into his incredible eyes. "I'm more contented than you will ever know."

"You are indeed a strange woman. I have heard many stories of how long it takes for a virgin to learn to enjoy bed sport."

He paused as though trying to remember something. "Last night, you promised to tell me how you know so much about lovemaking."

"And, as I recall, you said you would tell me why you are the one in my bed and not Charles and yet, I had to learn about it from your sister."

"Then you know the position into which I have been placed. Charles has made it very clear that during the nights you belong to me, but your days are reserved for him. I was sent to the stables as soon as I left your bedchamber this morning and told not to return until it was time for the evening meal."

Even though she knew what his answer would be, she remained silent, as though hearing the words for the first time. From the expression on his face, she knew he wasn't at all happy with her keeping secrets from him.

"I don't think I'm ready to reveal all of my secrets. In time I am certain you will know all about me. For now, let's just enjoy each other while we can." She knew her voice sounded sad but she couldn't help it. Somehow she had been transported to the past and a life she had only dreamed of living. Davida was afraid if she told anyone what had happened to her, somehow she would go back to her lonely existence in the twenty-first century.

As though Gwain completely understood her reluctance to speak of her past, he pulled her into a tender embrace and again started to bring her body to the point of full arousal. For however long it lasted, she would enjoy his attentions and savor the memory for the rest of her life.

41

Chapter Six

Davida awoke to her belly cramping. It had been so long since she'd experienced anything like this, and she was bewildered by the sensation. Had she eaten something that disagreed with her? Or was she merely reacting to the sexual activity that had been denied her for so long?

As soon as she sat up, she knew what was wrong. She was menstruating. The thought of it brought tears to her eyes. It would be days before she'd be able to be with Gwain. Being that the times were not modern, she would more than likely spend her days confined to this room.

A rap at the door prompted her to dry the tears that cascaded down her cheeks. To her relief it was Briana that entered the room. "Oh, Briana, I'm so glad it's you," she said before the tears again began to fall. "I'm afraid…"

"Oh dear, is it that you are bleeding?"

Davida nodded.

"I will be right back. Emma, the midwife, must be called. She will care for you. To be truthful, it is not a time for tears. I am always thrilled when it is my time and I do not have to be bothered with unwanted attentions from my husband."

Davida knew her sister-in-law meant well. Fred was so awkward at lovemaking that the few days her period lasted was a relief. With Gwain, it was an imposition. She would miss him terribly until he could again share her bed.

"Don't cry," Briana pleaded. "I know you thought that your lovemaking would plant a child. As a virgin, you had no way of knowing that sometimes it takes many cycles for a woman to carry a man's child."

Davida pretended to be ignorant of the workings of a woman's body. The first years of her marriage to Fred had been fraught with many months of infertility. Every period had become a time of grieving for the children that had not been conceived. She of all people knew there were only a few days of the month when a woman could get pregnant.

"I-I had hoped... I-I didn't think that my time for the cycle was so near."

"What you are feeling is natural. With the wedding, the days of travel, and the realization that Gwain would be the man in your bed, it is no wonder your time came when you least expected it. For the next few days, either Emma or one of the other women will be with you."

Davida lay back against the fluffy goose down pillows. Before menopause, her period was an inconvenience, but the world didn't stop because of it. She'd read about how in ancient cultures when a woman menstruated, she was treated with respect and care. How different it was in her time. In the twentieth and twenty-first centuries, life demanded that at that time of the month, a woman shoved a tampon up her box and went on as though the cramps, bad moods, and mess made those few days no different from any of the others in the month.

* * * *

Gwain was just finishing his morning meal when he saw Briana hurry toward the front door. He made no move to stop her, thinking that perhaps Davida had asked Briana to arrange for her to go riding when she finished eating.

"Where is Briana off to in such a hurry?" Charles asked, when he came to sit with Gwain.

"She didn't say."

Before Charles could comment, Briana returned with Emma, the midwife. When Emma climbed the stairs to the upper sleeping quarters, Briana joined them at the table.

"You were to be with Davida," Charles accused. "Why is it that the midwife goes toward her bedchamber while you sit here with us?"

"Davida awoke to her woman's flow. It is Emma's duty to comfort her during these days."

"Her woman's flow!" Charles shouted. "What have you been doing, Gwain? Why have you not gotten her with child?"

Charles pulled Gwain to his feet without allowing him to say a word. Once Gwain was upright, Charles landed a punch that sent him sprawling to the stone floor of the great room.

"You know nothing of women, Charles," Gwain said, as he got to his feet in order to defend himself. "It is too bad you were not fostered to our mother's brother along with me. If you had been, you would know that planting a child does not happen so close to a woman's flow."

"Do you expect me to believe such swill?" Charles retorted. "Have you been holding back your seed so that you can prolong your time with her? How can a virgin have such control over you?"

"Stop it, Charles!" Briana demanded. "Gwain is right. All you ever think of is fighting and war. If you took the time to listen to the women of this clan, you would know that a woman doesn't get with child every time a man shoves his cock into her. With everything this poor girl has endured, it may be months before a child can be planted."

Gwain smiled at the thought of several months of sexual bliss in Davida's room. Even when she did carry his child, his uncle had told him that no harm would come to the babe if he continued to enjoy Davida's pleasures.

"What do you know of the things Davida has endured?" Charles shouted, breaking Gwain's train of thought.

"I know that you arrived at her uncle's manor on her wedding day and killed the man she was to wed. After that you forced her to ride across the countryside in an open wagon with only Ian for company. I've known the man all my life and would sooner ride with a rabid dog than that man."

"How do you know of this?"

Gwain watched as a bewitching smile crossed his sister's lips. She was enjoying tormenting Charles with any knowledge she had about the way he had treated Davida on the trip from her uncle's home to McGowen Manor.

"My husband rode with you. Do you think he only fucks me at night? We do talk to each other, and the story of you killing the man she loved is too good to be kept secret. Every woman who has a husband who rode with you knows of it. Most of the men of the clan know that if they do not tell their wives what they want to know, their marital rights will be withheld.

Gwain watched as Charles clenched and unclenched his fists. Gwain had only been in Charles' company for a minimum of the time he'd been reunited with the clan, but he was well aware of his brother's temper. It was evident that Charles wanted to strike their sister.

In an attempt to save Briana from the brunt of Charles' anger, Gwain reached out to stop the blow that was certain to come.

"Do not stop him, Gwain," Briana said, her tone one of defiance. "He has no right to strike me. Word of such an action would endanger his standing with the clan. None but my own husband has the right to strike me, and he knows better than to test my anger."

Rather than admit to being bested by a mere woman, Charles stormed from the room, lashing out at any and all who got in his way.

* * * *

Davida wished she had a tampon to stop the flow that kept her confined to bed. She knew that in this time period men feared a bleeding woman. The only blood they tolerated was that of a virgin.

Before she could come to any concrete solutions about her situation, there was a knock at her door. Without waiting for anyone to bid her entry, an older woman came into the room.

"I am Emma, the midwife. Briana tells me you require my skills. When did you begin to bleed?"

"It must have been during the night."

"Of course, you know it is natural. In this household, it is my duty to make the time of your cycle more pleasant. Was it so in your uncle's home?"

Davida knew she had to think fast. The only experience she had with having her period came many centuries into the future. She couldn't say that she shoved a piece of tightly packed cotton up her cunt and went about her business as though it was any other day. She took a deep

45

breath and allowed a believable lie to pass her lips. "My nurse cared for me. We left in such a rush I never thought to request that she accompany me."

Emma clucked her tongue as she dipped warm water from the container that stood in the corner of her hearth. "You are one of us now, child. My daughters and I care for all the women of this clan during their confinements, be it their woman's cycle or the birth of their children and the time thereafter. It is a skill that I learned from my mother, as she did from her mother. It has been so for many generations and will be continued by my daughters long after I am gone."

Davida relaxed and allowed Emma to cleanse her body, apply fresh padding between her legs, and put fresh linens on the bed. She had to admit the treatment she was receiving from Emma far exceeded the way she'd handled her period in the twentieth century before menopause took that mess away forever.

"This certainly came at an inopportune time," Davida commented. As soon as she spoke, she realized how modern her words sounded.

"I'm afraid I don't understand the meaning of your words, lass."

"I'm sorry. We had many visitors to my uncle's home and from them I picked up many words that are different. I have always been fascinated by listening to their conversations with my uncle."

Emma rolled her eyes. "Listening to the conversation of men is not something that is tolerated here. You should be more interested in the running of the household and your sewing. Of course, I do not believe for one minute you are dwelling on your former life. I think you long for the time you will miss with your new husband. It takes a special lass to appreciate the lustiness of these McGowen men."

Davida smiled weakly, all the time wondering if Emma knew which McGowen brother graced her bed. It seemed as though Emma contemplated the very thing Davida was thinking about.

For a moment she thought about the woman who was to take care of her during the days of her period. Although she looked like an old crone, Davida knew Emma was, in all likelihood, no more than thirty-five, or forty years old. It was strange that she looked and acted much older than the twenty-first century Denise.

When Emma returned to the bedside, she brought Davida a cup of herbal tea. *How different this is from what I remember. It is possible that this tea will make these terrible cramps go away. It's a shame I didn't know about this when Fred and I were first married. It certainly would have stopped a lot of the fights we had.*

Chapter Seven

Snow fell early, confining Gwain to the great hall. Since the morning Emma had rushed to Davida's bedchamber, he had given his brother a wide berth.

From the corner of his eye, he saw Emma descend the stairs. She stood and exchanged words with Charles before leaving the hall to go to her own cottage. Her departure could only mean one thing. Davida had passed through the time of her woman's flow.

The thought no more than crossed his mind when Davida came down the stairs and took her place at the high table. She looked so radiant he wanted to take her to bed with no thought that it was but morning and the day belonged to Charles.

Before he could act on his intention, Charles was at Davida's side. The way he nuzzled Davida's neck made Gwain's cock strain to stand at attention. It was a shame that his brother could not enjoy the delights of Davida's body.

In the training he'd received during his fostering, Gwain had bedded many women. At his uncle's manor, the lasses were more than willing to spread their legs to accommodate his cock when it had been untried, as well as after his training. None of them had satisfied him in the way Davida did. After only two nights in her bed, he was hopelessly in love with the beautiful woman who belonged to his brother.

"I have ways to ease the ache in your cock."

Gwain looked up to see that Brian had taken a seat beside him. "I'm not my brother," he said through clenched teeth.

"Until you have been with a man, you should not judge the extent of

48

pleasure one can give. Since I was never interested in women, my father fostered me to a man he had known when he fought for Scotland. He taught me well, both in the art of war as well as that of love. You see, you and I are not much different, are we?"

Gwain swallowed hard. As much as he hated the words Brian spoke, he knew they rang true. Both he and Brian had been fostered far from their families. Like Brian, he had been instructed in the art of lovemaking. The only difference was that each had been trained to give pleasure to a different sex.

During his time with his uncle, Gwain had learned that there were men who were trained to relieve the sexual tension of the soldiers. Even with this knowledge, he never expected to have such a person living at McGowen Manor.

* * * *

Davida took her seat at the high table. Charles sat beside her, his presence casting an overpowering feeling of unease over her.

"It is good to see you back by my side, my love," he said. "I have missed you during your confinement. I pray that the next time you are confined to your chamber will be when you have delivered my son."

"I, too, pray that a child will be planted in my belly." She knew how hollow the words sounded, at least to her.

She and Fred had been disappointed so many times, but they had loved each other despite the disappointment and had not allowed it to destroy their marriage. From the things she'd heard since she arrived at the manor house, Charles had a terrible temper. If her barrenness followed her through the five hundred years she'd traveled into the past, could she continue to stay here and not be in danger?

Not if I am barren in 1470 as I was in 1970. Oh dear God, I know I prayed that I'd get pregnant when I was Denise, but it wasn't as important as it is now. If Davida doesn't get knocked up, I fear for her life at Charles' hand.

The pressure of her husband's hand on her knee told her of the pain he could inflict if things didn't go his way. Regardless of the pain he was inflicting, she looked up at him lovingly. She realized that she needed to put on a show for the clan. Her only consolation was that Gwain would be there at night to give her the love Charles reserved for Brian.

She glanced up in time for her eyes to meet Gwain's loving gaze. After what Charles said, she understood why he had chosen Gwain to be the man to father the next heir who would be the head of the clan.

As soon as their eyes met, Gwain looked away. Even though Davida knew this was the part he had to play, it bothered her. She hated the fact that she could only admit to the relationship in the privacy of their bedchamber.

"Return your attention to me, Davida," Charles warned. "I am your husband and to the clan I am also your lover. Your son will call me Father. Once the boy is named, Gwain will no longer be welcome in my home.

"And where does that leave me?" she hissed. "Would you condemn me to a loveless life, while Brian takes care of all your sexual needs?"

"Ah, my love, you have only just been awakened sexually. Once you have given me my son, you will thank me for relieving you of your wifely duties. It is a well-known fact that women do not enjoy the attentions of their husbands. In time you will know I have done you a great favor. At least you will not have to be concerned with which whore I take to my bed, as my mother was with my father."

Davida wanted to scream that she loved sex as much in this life as she had in the twenty-first century. The woman who now enjoyed her modern life may have been a virgin, but in her place Davida knew more about sex than her so-called husband. Before the swap, she had read everything from the Kama Sutra to Triple-X erotica. Even though Gwain was a practiced lover, she was certain she could show him many new tricks.

* * * *

Gwain enjoyed making eye contact with Davida, even though it was for only a moment. By the look on his brother's face, he knew Charles had chastised Davida for her diverted attention.

He had heard about Charles' temper but had yet to see it firsthand until he came home. For a fleeting moment, he saw Brian in a fresh light.

"Is my brother a considerate lover?" he asked, as he turned to face Brian.

50

"It is not a relationship built on consideration. Charles needs me to ease the ache in his cock and I need his protection. Men such as me are not accepted in most households. My training has prepared me to deal with men like Charles."

"Then why don't you leave?"

"Where else would I go? I don't expect you to understand. Charles accepts me for whom and what I am. The only thing that is expected of me is to keep him happy."

"Don't you want to be happy?"

"I learned early in life that someone like me performs a service for men who do not crave the feel of a woman's body. These men are angry with the lot they have drawn in life. I don't blame them. If that anger manifests itself in violence, it is something I am trained to deal with."

"Do you think he will become violent with Davida?"

"Not if she doesn't cross him. That is why I am here. When Davida began her confinement, Charles was very angry. He said that perhaps you were not man enough to get her with child. I tried to quell his anger and it looks as though my actions work."

"Do you call that working?" Gwain hissed. "Even here, in full view of the clan, he has somehow inflicted pain on her. I can see it in her eyes."

"The pain you see is but a warning. If he were to act upon his anger it would be with me, and I know how to control and extinguish it."

Gwain could stand to hear no more. His brother was a cruel man. He couldn't help but wonder whether he would be as cruel if he too had been raised in this manner. Rather than stay in the great hall, Gwain excused himself and went out to the stable. Riding in the cold crisp winter air would clear his mind of the evil sights and sounds of this manor house.

"Ye are Gwain McGowen, are ye not?"

The sound of a woman's voice coming from one of the empty stalls startled Gwain.

"Who is there?" he shouted.

"There is no need to shout at me," the woman said, as she stepped from the stall. "I am old but my hearing is not impaired. Now, will ye answer my question? Are ye Gwain McGowen?"

51

"I am, although I don't know what business it is of yours. Who are you to be asking me such a question?"

"My name is of no consequence to you. What I need to tell you involves Davida. Come to me at the deserted woodcutter's cottage by the lake tomorrow after you finish your morning meal."

Gwain grabbed at the woman's rag-covered arm, but she moved with surprising speed away from him. "Why can't you tell me what you have to say here and now? Why do you insist I wait until tomorrow and then go to the woodcutter's cottage?"

"Because what I have to say to you is for your ears only. There, I know no one else will overhear what you and you alone must know."

Before he could answer the woman she disappeared. He had not seen her leave the stable, but a search of all the stalls assured him she was nowhere to be found. He knew that he would think about what she had said throughout the day. Perhaps when he got to the cottage, there would be no one there. Considering the way she appeared and disappeared, it was entirely possible that he imagined the conversation.

Do not try to figure out what you have seen, the old woman's voice sounded in his mind. *It will all make sense when you come to the woodcutter's cottage tomorrow.*

* * * *

Davida watched Gwain leave the hall. Even though she knew that during the day she was to act the part of Charles' wife, she hated being alone with him.

"Do you ride, my dear?"

Charles' question brought to mind the saddle horses she and Fred once owned and boarded for many years. Never had she felt more at ease than when she donned her jeans and boots to take a weekend ride. As soon as the thought crossed her mind, she realized Charles expected her to ride in a dress. She'd read about ladies riding sidesaddle, but never thought she'd have to master the art.

"Do you mean as in riding a horse?" she finally managed to ask.

"What else would you ride?"

Oh, I could think of an answer that would curl this Scott's hair, but I don't think he means Gwain's cock. She knew she had to think before she spoke, or she could really be in trouble. "I thought perhaps a carriage."

"You are so refreshing. I expected you to be a suitable mate, but you are so much more. You are not only a beautiful woman, but you have a delightful childlike quality I enjoy. I have a very gentle mare and the saddle is one that I had handcrafted for you in London. I want to show you McGowen Manor, and the only way to do that is by horseback. It will be my pleasure to teach you to ride."

The sound of Charles' voice stood in direct contrast to the iron grip of his hand on her knee only moments earlier. She made a mental note to ask Gwain about it when they were alone. How could this man sound so gentle, yet be so cruel?

With the morning meal finished, Charles went out to the stable while Davida sought out Briana. Considering the snow that covered the ground, she would need warmer clothing if she were to go riding. She found Briana in the kitchen. "Can you help me?" she asked.

"What do you need help with?" Briana questioned.

"Charles wants to take me riding, but I fear I am not dressed for the cold."

"Did you ride in your uncle's home?"

The lie burned on Davida's tongue, but to admit to knowing how to ride might be her downfall. In this time period, women did not ride astride, and she didn't know how to ride sidesaddle. "No, but Charles said he would teach me."

"Charles wants you to be dependent on him. Be careful when you are with him. Even though he has entrusted the status of husband to our brother, he is jealous of the two of you. He wants that which he has relinquished to Gwain."

Davida agreed with Briana but held her tongue. To say too much would not be in her best interests.

"Come with me," Briana said as she took Davida's arm. "When I go riding in the cold weather I wear a pair of leather leggings that I made for myself. We will go to my bedchamber and find them for you."

Davida followed Briana to the bedchamber. Once there, she smiled at the soft, well-tanned doe skin. She pulled them on and fastened them tight with the drawstring at the waist. They were even more comfortable than her well broken-in jeans.

"I sense you are concerned about going riding," Briana said.

"I told you a bit of a fib. I have been riding, but never with a woman's saddle. I was a child when I rode the horses at my uncle's home and then I rode astride. I can only assume it will be…"

The look on Briana's face was one of bewilderment. "Why would you think of riding sidesaddle? No woman of this clan would consider riding in such a manner. It is something the English say is proper, but nothing we would do."

"I must have jumped to conclusions when Charles said that he had the saddle crafted for me in London."

"That puts a new light on the matter. If Charles has, indeed, sent for a saddle from England, it could well be an English sidesaddle. If that be the case, refuse to use it. I can only imagine what he would do to you once you were seated on it."

Armed with the information Briana gave her, Davida put on a heavy cloak and mittens that Briana called hand-muffs, and went out to the stables.

Charles waited for her. He held the lead rope for a beautiful chestnut mare that reminded her of her horse, Dolly. As much as being alone with Charles frightened her, the sight of the sidesaddle frightened her more.

"The mare is beautiful," she said, stroking the nose of the horse. "Have you named her?"

Charles stepped close to her, pressing hard against her backside. He put his hands against the horse's neck in order to trap her in his embrace. She wriggled to free herself from his attentions. Instead of freedom, he pulled her into his arms. "You are my wife," he hissed in her ear. "Never forget that you belong to me."

Davida's twenty-first century mentality boiled to the surface. Before she took time to think of what she said, words bubbled from her lips like water from an artesian well. "I belong to no man," she spat. As soon as she spoke the words and realized what she'd said, she regretted speaking without thinking.

In a movement that caught Davida off guard, Charles turned her to face him. "You are a spoiled bitch. I've broken the spirit of more than one bitch dog who thought she could bite her master. I will break you as well. You are but a woman and one, I might add, who thinks too highly of herself."

His hand reached under her cloak until he touched her breast. Rather than the gentle touch she'd come to expect from Gwain, Charles squeezed the globe until the pain became unbearable. When she grimaced, he pinched her nipple until she couldn't help but scream in agony.

"What are you doing to her?" Gwain's question sounded over Davida's screams, causing her to go limp.

"What I do to and with my wife is of no concern of yours," Charles snapped. "Nothing that transpires between the two of us during the day is for you to criticize."

Davida watched as Gwain clasped Charles' shoulder with his hand. In one swift movement, he pulled Charles away from Davida.

"Everything that transpires between you and Davida is of concern to me. You have entrusted her to me. You know war, Charles, but I know women. When a woman is upset, the chances of conception decrease. You want an heir, and yet you allow your temper to get in the way of it happening."

Charles backed away and Davida breathed a sigh of relief. "Charles is taking me riding," she said, addressing her comment to Gwain.

"Riding? On *that*? What are you thinking of, Charles? There's not a woman in the entire clan who would ride on that English abomination. Since Davida is now of our clan, she should ride as a clanswoman."

"The lass is not dressed to ride astride," Charles countered.

"Oh, but I am, Charles," Davida announced as she lifted her skirt to reveal Briana's leggings.

"What manner of dress is this?" Charles demanded, as he lifted her skirt up to her waist.

"They are leggings, much like the britches you wear," Davida replied, as she nodded toward the leather pants encasing Charles' legs. "If you will get me a proper saddle, I'd be pleased to go riding with you."

Charles grumbled as he pulled the sidesaddle from the back of the mare, while Gwain brought a more suitable saddle from the stable.

Davida smiled. She had won a minor battle. When she finally

mounted the horse, she pretended to listen to what Charles told her about riding. There was no need to lose the war by giving him cause to distrust her even further.

They started out slowly, but the exhilaration of being on a horse again urged her to kick the mare into a full gallop.

"What are you trying to do, kill yourself?" Charles questioned when he caught up with her. "You could have been thrown."

"But I wasn't," Davida replied, her eyes downcast. "What I did just came naturally. I'm sorry if I gave you cause for concern. I find I rather enjoy riding."

From the look on Charles' face, she knew she'd made another almost fatal mistake. She would need to be more careful in the future. She had to admit she enjoyed the freedom riding the mare had given her. Being able to ride would be one of the highlights of her life in this time period. Especially when Gwain was no longer her nighttime companion.

Chapter Eight

Gwain had come to the conclusion that Davida wasn't as naïve about sex as he'd been led to believe. There was no doubt she'd been a virgin when he came to her bed, but the way she'd received him told him she knew more than any woman he'd ever been with.

His thoughts brought to mind Athena. She told him that as a child she'd been the daughter of a nobleman and his mistress. When her mother died giving her life, her father had taken her to a house where she was trained to please men.

Athena had been a good teacher. Many of the things she had shown Gwain were duplicated by Davida. Could it be that she, too, had been trained in such a manner when her father died?"

"Gwain?"

The sound of his brother's voice calling his name interrupted his thoughts. "Yes, Charles," he replied as Charles came to his side.

"What is she like?"

"She?"

"You know of whom I speak. Is she as harsh in bed as she is whenever I am near her?"

The thought of Davida in his bed made Gwain harden with desire. "I shed her virgin's blood, but when I did, she became a beautiful temptress. She is as knowledgeable as Athena."

"Ah, you have told me of her. She is the woman who our uncle bought to train you."

"You make her sound like a common slave. When our uncle bought her, he immediately freed her. In return, she agreed to be my tutor as

57

well as give pleasure to our uncle. She taught me well in the same manner as she was trained."

"Then how is it that Davida is so knowledgeable? You assured me she was a virgin."

"And she was. I know not where she has acquired this knowledge. There is something she refuses to tell me of her past. Even so, I do intend to find out."

"How will you get her to tell you her secrets?"

"I feel that after tonight she will be more willing to talk to me. I plan to teach her a game of pleasure and trust."

"I want to be in the room with you tonight. I want to see that which I can only touch when she is by my side. Even if I cannot enjoy her as other men enjoy their wives, I do want to see her womanly attributes for myself."

Charles' request caught Gwain unaware. "Ordinarily, I would not agree to such a thing, since I am afraid it would be very upsetting to her."

"It is my right as her husband!" Charles shouted.

"You gave up those rights when you brought me here to give you an heir. I do not blame you for wanting to gaze upon her beautiful body. If you would have let me finish what I was saying, I would have told you that tonight will be a perfect time for you to join us, as she will be blindfolded and bound for the game of trust and pleasuring I have in mind."

"Why must you blindfold and bind her?" Charles asked, as though suddenly concerned for the safety of the wife he claimed in name only.

"Because she is too intent on giving pleasure. It is time to teach her to enjoy pleasure as well."

"I know this is how our uncle trained you, but I don't know if binding her will teach her the lessons of obedience you intend. Everyone knows women need to be beat in order to learn to obey their husbands."

"Not everyone thinks the way you do. In my world, women are cherished, not beaten. I do not intend to teach her to obey, but to learn to trust and enjoy. That is why you cannot enter her bedchamber until she is blindfolded. That way she will not know you are there. I will teach her to trust me not to harm her and at the same time give her more pleasure than most women receive in a lifetime. If you watch me, you will learn new ways to pleasure Brian. Be it man and woman or man and man, pleasure must be mutual."

"I have never thought of giving pleasure to Brian. He seems to be so..."

"He is human, and all humans deserve to be loved in return. It is his job to take care of your needs, but he has needs as well. Try to give him pleasure and perhaps he will not be quite so surly with the servants, to say nothing of the rest of the clan."

Charles nodded and proceeded to make arrangements to enter the bedchamber when Gwain told him it would be appropriate for him to do so.

* * * *

Davida finished her bath and dressed in a comfortable sleeping gown. The fire blazed brightly in the grate, illuminating the room. She knew she should light the candles, but the glow of the fire was more romantic. In all the books she'd read, she always loved the scenes where the hero and heroine made love by firelight.

It was one of many pleasures she never enjoyed with Fred. No matter how many times she pleaded with him to try different positions, he always insisted on making love the same way, under the covers and in the dark.

I don't know how this happened, but I've been given a second chance at love. If this is a dream, I hope I don't wake up.

Davida was so deep in thought she didn't hear Gwain enter the room until a shadow fell across the hearth. She looked up to see Gwain staring at her lovingly.

"I didn't think tonight would ever come," he said. "Your confinement seemed to make time drag for me. I thought the four days would never end." He held out his hands and helped her to her feet. Once they stood, eye to eye, he pulled her into his embrace and kissed her with a hunger that matched her own.

"I ached to have you hold me when Charles took me riding this morning," she whispered against his ear. The words prompted him to pull her even closer until he crushed her breasts against his chest. Even

59

with the material of her sleeping gown between them, she could feel the shivers of desire rushing to the lower portion of her body. More than anything else in the world, she wanted to make love to him through the hour of darkness.

To her dismay, he pulled away. "As much as I want to make love to you, we need to talk." He took her hand and led her to the bed.

"What is there to say?" she asked, confused by his sudden change in attitude.

Before answering, he sat down next to her and pulled her into a loving embrace. "I have told you that I was trained in all the arts of lovemaking. In my training I learned that a woman is only able to conceive at certain times of each month. My teacher was a beautiful woman by the name of Athena. In her native country she was trained to be a companion of men."

"A courtesan?" Davida asked. She'd read about them in *Glory and the Lightning* by Taylor Caldwell. She thought they were part of the ancient world. To hear Gwain describe Athena, she realized that even in 1470 such women were still being trained.

"Yes, she called herself a courtesan. I had no idea what that meant, but she soon taught me things I never dreamed possible. Now I want to teach them to you. One of her lessons was that love games are exciting and stimulating preludes to sex. Would you enjoy playing such a game tonight?"

Davida thought for a moment. Love games were nothing she'd ever experienced. It would be fun to pretend she was a courtesan. "I know nothing of these love games of which you speak. I wouldn't know what to do."

Gwain laughed at her statement. "This game is to teach you restraint. It is meant to teach you that pleasure given by one partner does not always have to be returned. It was a hard lesson for me to learn. I wanted to pleasure Athena for what she did for me. She informed me that I needed to learn to enjoy that which was given to me as a gift of love."

She watched as he reached behind them to retrieve a small backpack she hadn't noticed on the bed earlier. She could feel her clit begin to throb with excitement when he pulled out four silken cords and a blindfold. She recalled reading books about bondage that brought her close to an organism every time she read them. "Are those for me?" she asked, trying to sound innocent. "Do you plan to bind me?"

Gwain nodded. "Before I do, I want to see your naked body in the firelight." He reached down to the hem of her gown and pulled it over her head.

Just having his hands so close to her body made her wet with anticipation. Once she stood in front of him without the benefit of clothing, she allowed him to run his hands over her entire body.

As much as she wanted to touch him in return and drop to her knees to suck his cock, she restrained. He had told her tonight would be a lesson in restraint. No matter how much she wanted to feel him in her hands as well as her body, she made no such moves.

"You are responding well," he assured her as he tweaked her nipples with his thumbs. "I will bind you for the rest of your lesson."

He helped her to lie down on the bed and looped the silken cords around her ankles and wrists before securing them to the four posters of the bed. She giggled in anticipation of what he had in mind.

Before he put the blindfold in place, he undressed in front of her. With his cock in full arousal, she gasped in anticipation of the night to come.

Davida was beginning to enjoy Gwain's game of captive and captor until he picked up the silken scarf and tied it around her eyes. Suddenly, she was four years old and afraid of the dark. She'd never admitted her fear of the dark to anyone, not even Fred. It was the reason she always fell asleep with the television on. As the darkness engulfed her, she began to tremble. If only she could get the words past the cold hand of fear that clutched at her throat, she would tell Gwain to take the blindfold off and end this terror.

"Relax," Gwain said, his voice piercing the darkness. "This is a lesson in trust and pleasure. Do you trust me, Davida?"

Still unable to speak, she nodded her head. As soon as she did, something soft caressed her right inner thigh. The sensation was so erotic she fought her fears and began to moan softly.

* * * *

Gwain put the blindfold in place and nodded to Charles. He knew

61

his brother watched from behind the partially closed door. For a big man, Gwain marveled at how quietly Charles moved.

Instead of acknowledging Charles, he turned his attention back to Davida. She trembled as though the dark frightened her. "Relax," he whispered. "This is a lesson in trust and pleasure. Do you trust me, Davida?"

He expected her to speak. Instead she nodded. He couldn't help but wonder if she sensed Charles' entrance into the room.

A glance at his brother told him Charles was enjoying Davida's naked body, tied spread-eagle to the bed. Trying to ignore Charles, Gwain picked up the feather and trained it up Davida's inner thigh. As soon as he touched her, he could see her relax. Her moan of pleasure told him she was beginning to enjoy his love game.

The feather, he knew brought pleasures beyond belief. He flicked it over her puckered nipples as well as other erotic zones before moving it to the sensitive area around her clit. As soon as he touched her there, her woman's soul grew to a hardened nub and her nether-lips began to weep their milky love juices.

"Oh, Gwain, I can't take any more of this pleasure. Take me now."

He knew Charles wanted to stay, but they had agreed that what transpired between Gwain and Davida in bed was between them and not to be watched. As quietly as he entered the room, Charles left.

Once Gwain was certain he and Davida were alone, he removed the blindfold. To his surprise it was soaked with her tears. "Were your tears those of sadness or joy?"

"Both," she confessed. "I've always been afraid of the dark; those were the tears of sadness. What you did to me brought on tears of joy."

"I plan to give you many more tears of joy," he said as he straddled her prone body.

"Aren't you going to release me?"

"Not just yet. I rather enjoy having you at my mercy, and I think you are enjoying it as well."

* * * *

Davida knew exactly what he meant. She was at his mercy and her body was responding as though this was as normal as apple pie. *Just wait until you're at my mercy and see how you like being trussed up like a Thanksgiving turkey, buster. At least the blindfold is gone.*

Without giving her time to answer his statement, Gwain captured her lips with his own. The kiss was hot, his tongue probing. If the delightful pleasure he'd given her before hadn't been enough to make her pussy so hot she thought it would explode, this made her even hotter. She could feel her juices pooling and her clit throbbing and all he was doing was kissing her.

In all her life she'd never been kissed in such a fashion. Fred was content to pucker up and plant one on her lips as he ran out the door to work in the morning. If she wanted a kiss before going to bed, she usually had to ask for one. It was probably the fact that they'd been married for over thirty years. Longevity seemed to do that to a marriage.

She stopped thinking about Fred. It would do no good. He was long dead and she was far in the past with a bed partner to end all bed partners. Gwain was, indeed, a practiced lover who could drive her to the heights of passion with just a kiss.

As though he seemed satisfied with bringing her to the point of shuddering with desire, Gwain loosened his lip-lock and began kissing her neck. His kisses trailed down her chest until he was at her right breast. She never thought kisses would be so erotic, but they were driving her crazy. In a return to reality, he took her left breast in his hand and caressed her nipple while sucking her right breast noisily. While he did, his tongue swirled around her nipple and the sensitive area around it until she squirmed with delight.

After what seemed like an eternity, he released her breasts and moved further down her belly. His final destination was entirely clear when he took her clit in his mouth and sucked on it as he had her breast. This was the most delightful torture she had ever endured. As much as she wanted it to stop, she never wanted it to end. To add to her excitement, he filled her pussy with two fingers of his right hand, without missing a beat with his tongue and mouth.

More than once she screamed out in excitement and delight. The verbalization of the degree of pleasure he was giving her made Gwain increase his ministrations. By the time he moved to a position where he could fill her with his cock, his tongue and fingers had filled every opening in her body.

When he slipped his fingers into her ass, she inhaled sharply. As he slipped them effortlessly in and out, she couldn't help but wonder what it would feel like to have his cock filling that particular orifice. She prayed that sometime in the future she would find out, but for now she only wanted him planted firmly in her pussy. Anything else would have been anticlimactic.

His velvet shaft slipped easily into her cunt and his movements brought her more fully toward the orgasm she desired. On the first night she had noticed that he wasn't circumcised as Fred had been. She couldn't believe the difference it made to have his shaft sliding in and out of the protective foreskin.

As he pumped against her, she could feel her body screaming for release from the restraints so she could clasp her legs around his waist and drive him even deeper inside of her. When they finally climaxed, it was together and with such force she thought she would surely die from the pleasure.

Still connected, he collapsed on top of her and again began kissing her lips. She knew if she had a mirror she would see how swollen the lips surrounding her mouth as well as the ones guarding her pussy had become.

She thought he had fallen asleep when he again began to grow inside of her. As though renewed by the brief period of rest, he began to pump against her once more until she came again and again.

"Now, my delightful slave. It is time for the punishment before we begin again," he said as he rolled from on top of her.

"Punishment?" she questioned. "What have I done to be punished?" The man made no sense whatsoever.

"My dear, this is a game of trust, remember. Athena told me, that all slaves are punished after they are pleasured, especially love slaves. It heightens the pleasure. Do you trust me to heighten your pleasure?"

"Do I have a choice?"

"Tonight, the choices are all mine and the pleasure is all yours. I am rather enjoying this game of bondage and pleasure. Now, I am going to untie you, but you are still mine to command and you will obey my every wish."

She giggled in anticipation of what he had planned for her next. It couldn't possibly be any more exciting than what he had done to her since he came to her bed hours earlier.

To her surprise, once he untied both of her hands from the bedposts, he tied them together with the silken cords. Again bound, he brought her to her feet and seated himself on the bed.

"Lay across my lap, my lovely. It is time for your punishment."

She was almost afraid to do as he asked, but at the same time afraid not to. In anticipation, she laid across his bare legs. She could feel her nipples being tickled by the stiff hairs of his legs and his cock and pubic hair pressing against her side. Even though she had an idea of what was coming, she was shocked when he first spanked her bare ass and then shoved his fingers deep inside of her.

"I want you to equate pain with pleasure," he said.

She couldn't help but wonder if this was something Athena had taught him or something he thought up on his own.

Again he withdrew his fingers and spanked her, this time sticking his fingers in her ass.

"You have a delightful ass. I can hardly wait to sink my manhood into its warm embrace."

"Then why don't you do it now?" she asked.

"Ah, but you are an adventurous lass. Tonight is not the night for such pleasure, for the pleasure would be all mine. I am afraid you would find the act distasteful, but in time you would come to enjoy it. For now I am more interested in your cunt than your ass. It is only fun to tease it."

With that said, he spanked her one more time before telling her to get to her feet. As soon as she looked down on him, she saw his cock standing at attention, larger and more tempting than ever. She was just about to drop to her knees to give him a blowjob when he pulled her onto his lap facing him, impaling her on him as though she were being impaled upon a spike in one of the medieval books she had read.

The pleasure he had given her so far tonight couldn't begin to measure up to this. His pubic hair caressed her clit as his cock filled her so far she thought it was tickling her tonsils. She wondered if it would have been this way if he hadn't spanked her. She had never felt anything so erotic as his hand connecting with her ass, followed by his fingers manipulating her until she was so wet with desire that she slid easily onto his cock.

Even though her hands were still tied, she managed to lock them securely behind his head and bring her mouth down on his. Imitating his earlier kisses, she slipped her tongue into his mouth over and over again, each thrust matching the ones she was making by moving her body up and down over his cock.

With the last orgasm, she knew she was completely spent. She allowed him to help her to her feet and then to lie down in bed. Again he tied her hands and feet to the bedposts. She couldn't help but wonder how much more of the pleasure she could stand.

She watched as he made his way to the hearth. When he returned it was with the soft clothes and warm water she knew he would use to cleanse her body. Like a kitten with its belly full, she purred as he cleansed her body from their lovemaking.

"Tomorrow night, my love, we will explore even more positions. I want to give you every ounce of pleasure that I can. If we are lucky, when the time is right we will plant a child beneath your breast. When we do, I will teach you all the delightful ways I can bring you to complete arousal, even when your belly is swollen with my child."

Tears formed in her eyes. "I don't want to be with child," she protested. "Once the child is born and named, I will no longer have you in my bed. After tonight, how can I even hope to live without your cock at my beck and call?"

"We will not think of that time. Perhaps, once the child is born it will be a girl and we will have to begin again in the attempt to make a boy child for my brother. If that is the case, I will look forward to enjoying your mother's milk, for Charles will undoubtedly had a wet nurse for her. It is a known fact that a nursing mother cannot conceive. I plan to keep your milk flowing until you are ready to have another child."

It's a nice thought but one that has been dispelled over the years. How else could women have children so close together? As I recall, my friend Connie had one nursing and another in the oven all at the same time. Once the new baby was born, they both nursed, so don't give me this crap about not being able to get knocked up when you're nursing.

Chapter Nine

Gwain thought he would sleep later after the night of lovemaking he'd enjoyed with Davida. Instead, with the first light of morning he was awake. As soon as he finished his morning meal, he would ride out to the woodcutter's cottage and meet the old crone he'd seen yesterday in the stable.

After his morning routine of washing and shaving he went down to the great hall. To his surprise, Charles waited for him.

"She is indeed beautiful," Charles greeted him. "She deserves to be loved."

"And when I leave, who will love her then?"

"She will have my son to care for. Women do not have the same urges and needs as men. She will be content to not have to perform her wifely duties."

"Does Brian take care of your urges for you?"

Charles nodded, causing Gwain to be sick to his stomach. The thought of two men satisfying each other in the same way he and Davida did was unnatural to him. "I am afraid you underestimate her urges. A child cannot warm a woman's bed at night. Would you deny my son the privilege of brothers and sisters?"

"I do not see that as a privilege. Briana is more of a bother than a joy. As for you and me, we didn't grow up together. I claim you as brother because of our bond by blood, but not by memories or shared experiences. What difference would it be with my son?"

"Your heir, Charles, not your son. He will always be of my seed. Although McGowen blood will flow through his veins, he will never be

67

yours."

Without waiting for Charles to respond, Gwain stormed from the hall. It was better to forgo the morning meal than to argue further with Charles.

"Where are ye off to, laddie?" Angus asked when Gwain almost knocked him over in his rush to leave the hall.

"As far away from Charles as I can get, Uncle."

"What of the morning meal?"

"I have lost my appetite. I prefer the company of my horse to that of my brother. I will return for the evening meal. By that time, both Charles and I will have put this morning's argument behind us." He knew Angus had more to say, but this was not the time for him to listen objectively.

The cold north wind did little to quell Gwain's anger. Even though he knew a storm was brewing, he made his way to the stable to get his horse. As soon as he entered the warmth of the building, the thought of going back out into the cold sent a shiver of dread up his spine.

He glanced into the empty stall where the old woman had been just one day earlier. Her words echoed in his head. *What I need to tell you involves Davida.*

Why didn't she tell me what she wanted yesterday? Why make me go out into the cold and brave the coming storm?

With no answers, Gwain saddled his horse and prepared for the ride to the woodcutter's cottage. Sleet stung his face as he led the horse from the stable. It was tempting to turn back to the manor house, but the old woman had insisted he come today. Whatever it was she had to tell him, he knew she'd planned this for today. Not to go would jeopardize his ever learning what she meant.

By the time he arrived at the woodcutter's cottage, the snow was falling heavily, obliterating his tracks from the manor house. Smoke curled from the chimney, encouraging Gwain to hurry toward the cottage. The very thought of the warmth represented by the blaze in the fireplace made him hurry toward his destination.

Once he saw to his horse, he knocked at the door of the cottage. His knuckles barely left the wood when the old crone opened the door.

"I thought perhaps you wouldn't come," she said as she stood to one side so that he could enter the room. "This storm is one of the worst I have ever seen."

"I was afraid if I did not come you would not tell me about Davida," Gwain replied.

The old woman stepped aside so that Gwain could enter the room to warm himself by the fire.

"Are you going to tell me who you are and how you know of me?"

"As I told you yesterday, my name is of no consequence. As for how I know of you, I could see you when I foretold Davida's future. Although I told her only of her marriage to Charles, I did see you in her future. At that time, she was in love with Robert and could not bear the thought of either his death or spending her life in a loveless marriage. She was ready to give herself to Robert, but not to Charles. She begged me to allow her to change places with a future reincarnation of herself."

The word reincarnation stunned Gwain. "That really happens?"

"Of course it does. The Davida you have loved and will continue to love is a woman from over five hundred years in the future. In that life her name is Denise. She is an experienced woman and a widow. In that time she is still a young woman, even though she has passed her fiftieth year. It is the reason you find her such an accomplished lover."

Gwain could hardly believe his ears. "In this future time, what is her life like?"

"People live longer and better. Sexuality is embraced and erotic pleasures are embraced. The Davida, who has now become Denise, is not comfortable with the things she is seeing. When the babe is born she wishes to return to her life as Charles' wife and care for the child. She knows that once the child is conceived and born she will no longer be expected to do anything but raise the child."

"And what will happen to the Davida I know?"

"She will return to her life with pleasant memories of all that has occurred in this time period. Unfortunately, the life she will return to will be without love, as her husband of many years has died. Unless she can find another to love, she will be destined to live out her life as a widow who only fantasizes about what loving a man is like. She will always cherish the memories of her life in this time period and the love she has shared with you. She will also carry fond memories of the child she gave birth to, for in the life she has led, she was barren."

"How will I live without her?"

"The same way you would have lived if she had remained here. Charles will ban you from the manor house and you will never see your son grow up. You will not meet again until you are a man and even then you will not be able to claim his as your own, for he will have grown up believing that Charles is his father. He will be more like Charles than you, for he will have been molded into the type of man Charles desires him to be."

"What am I to do?"

"Confront Davida with the truth. She knows what has happened to her and there will be many wondrous things she can tell you of the future. Once she is gone, there will be many other women in your life."

"But will I find the love I have found in her arms?"

"That is not for me to say. You must make your life for yourself. If you allow yourself to love, you will do so. If not, you will never be satisfied with this life."

"What can you tell me of my son?"

"He will be a man to make you proud. Although he will be a soldier, he will be the one to bring honor to the McGowen name. Those from far and near will know of him and he will be well-respected. He will lead the clan and no one will question his right to do so."

"What of Charles?"

"That is not for me to say, for he is but your brother and not your son. Only time will tell what his role in life is to be. My only warning is this: do not return to the manor house once your son is named. Even now Brian is poisoning Charles' mind against you. Your destiny lies neither at McGowen Manor nor in Scotland."

The old woman turned to stir a pot of stew, indicating that she had nothing more to say.

As Gwain prepared to leave, he realized that it was already dark and the storm raged so violently that going out in it would be too dangerous. Even though he had told Angus that he would return for the evening meal and he had promised Davida to share her bed this night, he knew neither would happen.

The aroma of the old woman's stew reminded him that he had eaten nothing since last night. His stomach growled in anticipation of the meal she would be serving him.

"I knew you would not be leaving here this night. I have prepared a bed for you and I know you are hungry. Eat your fill. Tomorrow will be soon enough for you to return to the manor. This storm will not abate until the wee hours between darkness and dawn."

"Did you know of this storm when you bid me come to you?"

The old woman gave him a toothless grin. "I did."

His anger began to grow. "You knew I would be stranded here and still you asked me to come. What manner of woman are you to deprive me of even one night in Davida's bed?"

"You needed to know the truth sooner rather than later. One night will make no difference, since she cannot conceive this night. You will have many nights of pleasure without the interruption of her woman's flow before she is taken from you. When the inevitable does happen it will set the course for all of your lives. Again and again you will cross paths throughout eternity. Now come and eat before you take your rest. The storm will blow itself out by morning and you will again return to your Davida. I do give you one warning. Learn all you can from her of the future, but be careful of what you tell her. The time is not right for her to know of her return to her own time."

* * * *

The howling of the wind made Davida glad to have the warmth of the heavy woolen clothing this time period forced her to wear. At breakfast she had heard Charles and Angus arguing about Gwain. From what she could gather, Charles and Gwain had quarreled and Gwain had gone out into the storm.

The heavy snowfall combined with the high winds to produce blizzard conditions and force everyone to remain inside. The men wrestled, played games of chance, and remained underfoot for the entire day. Throughout the day, she glanced often toward the door in the hope of seeing Gwain return. To her dismay, he didn't come to the noon meal.

By suppertime she had begun to worry. If she'd been in the twenty-first century, she would have been calling the state patrol as well as the hospitals. When he finally returned, she would have berated him for not calling to tell her where he was.

"I'm concerned about Gwain," Angus said, when he approached Charles at the high table. "He was in a foul mood when he left this morning. I just checked the stable and his horse is not there. It is possible he has become lost in the storm."

"And what would you have me do? Should I put more lives in danger? I care not what he does as long as he leaves me alone."

"Ye should care what happens to the lad. Without him, you will have no heir, or have you forgotten his position in this clan?"

"I forget nothing, Uncle Angus. Gwain is a grown man. If he has no more sense than to go out in a storm like this one, he has no one to blame but himself. His temper has gotten him into this mess. He is like a stray dog. He will return when hunger claws at his gut and not before."

"He could be lost and freezing," Davida insisted. "He could need you. Have you no compassion for your own brother?"

"Do not concern yourself with matters of this manor, Davida," Charles countered. "You know nothing of the relationship between Gwain and me."

"I know that he was fostered out to your uncle when he was but a boy and you know little of the man who should be one of your closest friends. It is sad." She started to get up to leave the table, but Charles' hand on her knee prevented it.

"You will not disgrace me by leaving this table before we have supped. Then and only then can you go to your room and sulk. Perhaps Brian and I can join you later and participate in the game Gwain taught you last night."

The mention of what had transpired between herself and Gwain the night before caused a shiver of dread to run through her body. "How...how could you know?"

"Once you were blindfolded, I entered your chamber and watched as Gwain gave you pleasure."

"How could you? How could *he*? That was private!"

"Nothing about you is private. You are my wife and as your husband I have certain rights and privileges. One of them is to see that which I can only feel and not enjoy. You have a beautiful body. My brother is indeed a lucky man."

"But I thought..."

"You thought I preferred men. Because of my injuries, I have learned to enjoy Brian's attentions. That does not mean I do not appreciate a beautiful woman. If I could enjoy and satisfy you in the way you deserve, you would have never known Gwain."

"The lot you have drawn in life is a difficult one to say the least. I am pleased you have such a loyal friend in your life. I pray you appreciate Brian and reward him generously."

"What do you know of what goes on between men?"

Davida weighed her answer well. *More than you think, Buster. I saw Brokeback Mountain and enough of my friends have gay sons so that I'm not ignorant of such things.* "Very little, but I have heard whispered conversations. Even as sheltered as I was, there were things I could not help but overhear. It is unnatural, but it is the way God made many men, and I believe He does not make mistakes."

She saw sorrow mirrored in Charles' eyes. "God did not make me this way," he said, just loud enough for her to hear.

"Not originally, but God controls everything in our lives. He even turns that which happens into the fate that rules us all. Do you think I do not know that my marriage to you was predestined, just as Robert was born to die young? Had he not died at your hand, something else would have taken his life."

"What manner of training have you had? I have never heard anyone explain the mystery of life and death in this fashion before."

"I have had no training. I only remember a man of God saying that God knows the number of breaths each living creature will take while it lives upon the earth. It stuck in my mind." *At least I didn't say I read it in the Bible. I won't make that mistake again.*

Supper was served to them, ending the conversation that had turned too philosophical for her taste. With the meal finished, Davida excused herself to go to her bedchamber. Since Gwain had not returned, she knew her bed would be lonely tonight.

Once alone in her room, she added more logs to the fire and sat down with her sewing. She silently thanked her grandmother for insisting she learn how to embroider, crochet, and knit, and her 4-H leader for teaching her to sew. The piece she picked up was a small gown for when the baby was born. She prayed that she would be able to conceive and know the joy of having Gwain's child grown in the hidden place beneath her breast.

A light rap at the door made her heart pound with anticipation. Perhaps Gwain had returned after all and she wouldn't be forced to spend the evening alone. She sat aside her sewing and got up to answer the door. To her surprise, Brian stood just beyond the threshold.

"May I come in?" he asked, when she stood speechless.

"Of course. I didn't expect to see you."

"As you should be. What was it you said to Charles while you sat at the high table?"

"We spoke of many things. Why do you ask?"

"Because, when the meal was finished, he took me to one side and thanked me for my loyalty to him. Never before has he acted in such a way. I am now on my way to our bedchamber. Before I reached the door, I saw one of the servants bringing us a bottle of good whiskey for our enjoyment this evening. The only thing I can attribute his change in manner to is something you might have told him."

Davida smiled. She remembered the conversation distinctly. Maybe this was the reason she changed places with the woman who should be in this time period. "All I said was that he was lucky to have such a good friend and lover in his life. I also said that he should reward you. I'm pleased he has seen fit to follow my advice."

Brian looked as though what she had just said was in a foreign language that he did not understand. "Are you saying you do not find our relationship objectionable?"

"What the two of you do when you are alone is not my affair. It is not something that I completely approve of, but I feel each man and woman must travel the path that is right for him or her. Since you make Charles happy, it is only right that he should appreciate and reward you. I know of his temper and pray that he will think twice before he loses it when he is with you."

To her surprise, Brian reached out to take her hand and press it to his lips. "You are, indeed, a gracious lady. Many wives would release their anger at this situation upon their husband's lover, be they male or female."

A point for me, she told herself, as she went back to her sewing. *I never thought I would be tolerant of a relationship like this, but why not? Charles is not the man I want in my bed. If he is able to be content in a relationship with Brian, so much the better. Now I must find a way to keep Gwain in my life after the child is born.*

As much as she wanted Gwain in her bed, she knew that this night she would be alone. She'd been alone ever since Fred died, so tonight wouldn't be much different from any of the nights that she's spent in the king-sized bed of her side of the duplex. Even before she'd been alone, she'd learned the skills of self-gratification and certainly wasn't too prudish to indulge her desires.

After undressing, she stood in front of the fire caressing her breasts. *That's right, baby, do it just as I taught you.* The sound of Fred's voice within the confines of her mind startled her.

"How?" she asked aloud.

I am able to monitor your thoughts and see what is happening in your life. This situation is strange, to say the least, but I must admit, Gwain is a much better lover than I was. Now listen to my instructions and do as I tell you.

At Fred's instruction, she continued to fondle her breasts and rub her thumbs over her sensitive nipples.

As she did, she could feel the love juices surging to her cunt and her clit throbbing with the ache that only the stimulation of a hand-job could release.

Sufficiently warmed by the fire, she slid her nightgown over her head and went to the soft bed where Gwain had taken her to the heights of pleasure just hours earlier.

Once in bed, she pulled the nightgown up over her ass and began to run her hands over her entire body. For a moment, she again played with her tits, paying equal attention to each nipple. Satisfied with the sensations coursing through her body, she moved her hands down her flat belly until her fingers were entangled in her pubic hair.

As she slipped her fingers in the hidden crevice, she manipulated the bud of her desire until her body jerked in forced release. She continued until she lost all sense of reality. In her present arousal, she decided that she would treat Gwain to an impromptu strip show when they were again together. She prayed he would enjoy it as much as Fred always did.

Chapter Ten

Gwain awoke, aware that he was alone in the cottage. He wondered where the old crone could have gone. After throwing off the blanket, he got up from the bed of fresh pine boughs the old woman had prepared for him last night. To his surprise, the fire that burned in the hearth warmed the cottage and a piss-pot stood in the corner for him to use.

It pleased him not to have to go outside to relieve the morning hard-on. In his dreams he'd been with Davida. He awakened with such an ache in his cock, he wished he could relieve it inside Davida and not the piss-pot.

"You're awake!"

He turned at the sound of the old woman's voice, and shoved his cock back into his britches as he did.

"I thought you left," he said, a bit more indignantly than he wanted to sound.

"I will leave soon but not until you're fed. Even though the storm has passed, it will take you most of the day to return to the manor house. The snow is deep and will make the ride back a long and tedious one. Add to that the cold and perhaps you would be wise to stay here until the weather warms a bit."

"Like hell I will. I have no desire to spend another night away from Davida. If what you have told me is true, she will be returning to the time from which you have snatched her and will be replaced by a woman I do not know."

"Suit yourself, but don't say I didn't warn you."

Even though Gwain knew exactly what the woman meant, he wasn't about to allow her to dictate his moves. He knew the wind had blown all night and he had no delusions about the depth of the snow. When he came yesterday the snow was already falling heavily. It would be slow going to return to the manor house. He also considered the cold, but how cold could it be? He'd lived most of his life at his uncle's estate, and there the snow was always followed by warm breezes from the ocean. It certainly wouldn't be much different here.

With a hot meal in his belly, he saddled his horse and began the trek back home. The thought of spending the night in Davida's arms warmed his body. As he continued to fantasize about her love, he remembered the old woman's story of how Davida had come from another time far in the future, when love was more open and women far more experienced. Just the thought of a society of women with Athena's expertise was enticing.

He wanted to urge his horse to a full gallop, but the snow was so deep that even a slow walk was difficult to maintain. At this pace, even the promise of Davida's love couldn't keep the cold from settling into his bones and stinging his face. He would be lucky to return to the manor house without freezing his hands and feet in the process. Coming here in spite of the storm had been foolish. As the thought crossed his mind, he couldn't help but remember that if he hadn't come, he wouldn't know of Davida's well-guarded secret.

* * * *

Davida had spent a restless night. Her concern over Gwain's absence, coupled with Charles' refusal to go out and search for his brother, kept any possibility of sleep at bay. With the first weak rays of sunlight that came through her window, she got up and started her morning ritual of washing her face in the warm water she kept by the hearth for her sponge bath. After dressing for the day, she made her way down to the great hall.

Upon entering the hall, she saw many people still sleeping on the mats that had been laid out in front of the fire. Neither Charles nor Brian was in sight, leaving her to believe they had shared a night of pleasure. The thought brought a smile to her lips at the memory of how she might have been instrumental in bringing that about.

Instead of taking a seat at the high table, she made her way to the kitchen to offer her help to the women who worked under Briana's supervision.

"I hate these storms," she heard Briana say. "My husband is as bad as a horny old goat when he can't get outside. He thinks I have nothing better to do than to fuck him all night and cater to his belly at first light, even though he won't get his lazy ass out of bed until the sun is high in the heavens. He thinks that just because he can't be doing whatever it is he does, I have nothing to do either."

Davida silently wished she had such a problem. Last night she'd been lonely. Even the masturbation that used to give her such pleasure hadn't stopped either her tears of loneliness or her ache of sexual need.

"I suppose you were well-fucked last night, Davida," Briana greeted her. "When it comes to sexual appetite, no man can come close to my brother."

Davida didn't dare raise her eyes to meet Briana's gaze. If she did, she knew she would break down and cry. "I spent the night alone."

Briana took her arm and led her to a corner away from the other women. "Did Gwain not return last night?"

Davida shook her head. "With the storm I'm concerned. Even Angus asked Charles to go out and search for Gwain, but he refused. I hope by the light of day he will return from wherever it was he spent the night."

"Do you think he was with another woman?"

"There is nothing I could say if he was. He is not my husband. He has no reason to remain faithful to me."

"I will speak to my husband. Perhaps he and some of the other men will go in search of him."

Davida shook her head. "I don't think it's wise to go against Charles' wishes. Angus and I have both had our say in this and it makes no difference to my husband. He and Gwain had a terrible argument. Perhaps he is having a problem accepting the fact that his heir will be Gwain's son."

"Why is the morning meal not on the table?" Charles bellowed from the great hall.

Around Davida, women scurried to put food on the platters and take it out to the high table. Instead of joining them, Davida filled a plate and sat in front of the fireplace the women used for cooking and that warmed the kitchen. The aroma of the wood fire, mingled with the grease from cooking, reminded her of when she spent the night with her grandmother on the farm. Even though her own mother had an electric range, Grandma insisted on using her woodstove for cooking. She contended she was too old for such newfangled gadgets.

Tears formed in her eyes and rolled down her cheeks. Just the thought of her grandmother brought to the forefront the losses she had suffered. Her parents had died in a car accident shortly after her wedding, her grandmother had passed away ten years ago, and she'd lost Fred eight years later. Other than her friends, she was completely alone. Maybe that was the reason she'd been transported to this time and place. There would be no one in the twenty-first century to miss her.

The feeling of loneliness filled her even more with the thought of Gwain spending the night with another woman. If he did not return here, there would be no child. She'd be left alone to face Charles' wrath. With neither Gwain nor his baby to love, she didn't know if she could survive.

Being alone, her silent tears turned to heart-wrenching sobs. She was on the verge of hysteria when she felt a man put his hand on her shoulder. Startled, she turned to stare into Charles' incredible green eyes.

"Why do you not take your morning meal at the high table?" he asked, his voice surprisingly soft.

She wiped away her tears with the back of her hand. "I would not be pleasant company this morning," she confessed.

"Would you join me if I promised to go out and look for Gwain when the meal is finished?"

His offer took her completely by surprise. "You'd do that?"

He nodded. "Your tears are evidence that you love him, even though the two of you have been together but for a short time. I cannot stand to see you so unhappy."

"Concerned, Charles," she corrected him. "I have lost so much in my life; I cannot abide the thought of another loss."

He pulled her to her feet and into his embrace so he could comfort her as she cried even harder. "Did you truly love this man you were prepared to marry when I finally found you?"

Davida nodded, unsure if the woman whose place she took was capable of love. The dream she'd had caused her to believe there had

79

been love, but of course it had also caused her to believe that Davida's virginity was no longer intact. She didn't know if she should put her trust in the dream that precipitated her transportation five hundred years into the past.

"Come with me," Charles said, as he put his arm around her shoulders and guided her toward the great hall. "You will feel better after you eat a proper meal."

If the people were surprised to see Charles bringing Davida to the high table, they didn't show it.

"Are ye all right, lass?" Angus asked.

Davida nodded.

"Several of the lads are ready to go with me in search of Gwain. Had Charles not ordered it, we would have done it on our own. It is not like Gwain to be gone overnight with no one knowing where he is. It is possible he got caught in the storm and found a cottage where he could ride it out. I'm certain no harm has come to him. Rest easy, lass, we will be bringing him safely home."

Angus patted her hand reassuringly as if to convince her of his sincerity. "Thank you, Uncle Angus. Charles' concern, coupled with yours, is comforting. I know you will find him."

* * * *

Gwain prayed he was going in the right direction. The frigid wind swirled the snow around him until he was uncertain where his horse was taking him. He could only hope the animal was headed in the direction of the manor house and his warm stall.

He squinted against the snow that blew into his face and stung his eyes. It was hard to tell if the snow was again falling or if it was merely doing the bidding of the wind.

In addition to losing his sense of direction, he'd lost all track of time. *Have I been riding for an hour or an entire day? Am I going in the right direction or am I completely lost?*

You have lost your way. The voice of the old woman sounded in his mind. *But those of your clan are searching for you at this very moment. Soon you will be reunited with your Davida. Savor your time with her, for soon you must come to a decision about your future.*

"Gwain, Gwain, where are yea, laddie?" The sound of Uncle Angus' voice silenced the old woman.

Am I dreaming? Do I only think I hear Angus calling my name?

Again he heard his uncle's voice. Unwilling to miss an opportunity for rescue, he called back. "I'm here." The weakness of his voice alerted him to the dire straits in which he found himself. The cold had robbed him not only of his senses but also of his voice.

In desperation, he tired to decide from which direction the sound of Angus' voice came. The wind had a way of playing tricks on those foolish enough to get caught out on a day like today, but he was certain Angus was to his right. If he continued in this direction they would never cross paths.

He pulled on the reins in order to turn his horse, but the beast was stubborn and refused to move. Unable to shout curses at him, he pulled harder on the reins. This time, the horse retaliated by rearing up. With his fingers numb from the cold, the unexpected actions of his horse unseated him and sent Gwain flying to the snow-covered ground. Beneath the fluffy snow, a rock lay hidden until Gwain hit his head on it.

Warm blackness replaced the biting cold that had been his enemy ever since he left the woodcutter's cottage and the old woman earlier in the day.

* * * *

Davida paced the great hall. Charles had eaten quickly and gone out with Angus and the other men to search for Gwain. She worried for the safety of all of them as the temperature had dropped far below zero and with the wind, being out for any amount of time was life-threatening.

If she'd been at home, it would have definitely been a day to stay inside. She could almost hear the news commentator saying that the temperature was so low that the wind-chill had hit forty below zero. She recalled days like this well. When winter hit with a vengeance, her car complained about starting and her garage door usually didn't want to go down without her help.

If her calculations were correct, it was somewhere close to Thanksgiving. Back home the hunters would be praying for snow, but storms like this didn't come until January at the earliest.

81

She closed her eyes and tried to remember her grade school geography. If she was correct, Scotland lay far north of Wisconsin, and from the length of time it had taken to come here from her Uncle's home, she was up close to what would be called the North Shore in the future.

She'd corresponded with a girl who moved to the Shetlands after her marriage and had read of the relentless winds and the cold of the area.

A gust of cold wind prompted Davida to turn toward the door. As she did, she saw the men who had left earlier enter the great hall, and they were carrying Gwain.

"Take him to Davida's chamber," Charles ordered. "It is the smallest and the easiest to heat."

Davida hurried to Charles' side. "Is he…" She couldn't finish.

"He's unconscious. He was thrown from his horse and hit his head. Luckily, he wasn't far from here. Since your chamber is already warm, it is the best place for him. I will come to help you as soon as I instruct the women to bring hot water for his bath."

The memory of going to a one-room rural school as a child assaulted Davida's mind. At the time there had been a family who was so poor the kids were sent to school without proper clothing. It had been a cold day when the boys came to school in tattered jackets and no socks or mittens. Their hands and feet were frostbitten. The older girls had wanted to heat water, but the teacher insisted they use water that was room temperature. It had worked and as far as she knew there'd been no permanent damage done to either brother.

"Not hot, Charles. The water should be tepid, closer to cool than hot," she said, her voice sounding authoritative.

"Cool water? Have you lost your mind, woman?"

"Please trust me. I know what I'm doing. Have the women send up four basins when they bring the water, and lots of clean towels as well as strips of clean linen for bandages. I will go and prepare a place for Gwain close to the fire. I will also need the help of three other people."

Without waiting for an answer, she hurried toward the stairs. After taking the steps as quickly as her long skirt allowed, she ran down the hall to her chamber. The fire she'd banked earlier burned brightly, and the room seemed much warmer than the rest of the manor.

A lounge chair sat against the far wall and she pulled it close to the fire and piled it high with the blankets from her bed. She'd just finished when the men entered the room, carrying Gwain.

"Put him on this lounger," she instructed. "When you have, help me take off his clothes."

"Take off his clothes?" Angus questioned.

"Yes. They're as cold as he is. We'll wrap him in these blankets and allow the heat from the fire to do the rest."

Without further questions, the men took off Gwain's shoes and stockings as well as his coat, leggings, and shirt. Naked, he shivered inadvertently but did not regain consciousness.

"What are you doing?" Charles demanded as he held open the door to allow the women access to the chamber with the basins as well as the container of water.

Davida continued to wrap the blankets around Gwain's body. "I asked you to trust me," she said without diverting her attention from Gwain. "Place a pan next to each of his hands as well as his feet and fill them with the water. With him unconscious it will not be an easy task, but we must immerse his hands and feet in the water."

Charles asked no further questions but instead hurried to do as she told him. She watched as the men bent Gwain's knees so that his feet could be put in the basin. The men who took up the positions at his sides held his hands in the water as well. While others took care of his hands and feet, Davida put soft clothes into the water and packed them around his face. With that done, she washed and assessed the cut on the back of his head. She was relieved to find that it was minor even though it would require at least a couple of stitches. Carefully, she washed the frozen blood from his hair and thanked God that due to the cold, the bleeding hadn't been as bad as she expected.

She wasn't at all certain as to how to go about stitching shut the wound, but she did know the needle needed to be sterilized. She chose a needle and silken thread from her sewing box. Before she was ready to begin, Emma entered the room. It relieved Davida when the older woman took the needle and thread from her hands.

"I will take care of his wound, lassie," Emma said. "You need to make certain these men do as you tell them."

Davida gladly relinquished the task she so dreaded and went to check on each man in turn. She was pleased to see the color returning to Gwain's skin, even if it was turning bright red. She knew that blisters would soon be forming. She prayed she would know what to do when that happened.

After instructing the man to dump the now cold water and refill the bowl with fresh water, she dried Gwain's hand. The blister that she worried about was already starting to form, even though his skin was still cold to the touch.

"Is there anything else you require?" Emma asked, before Davida moved to the basin of water that held Gwain's right foot.

"Even though he is unconscious, he must drink hot tea. It will warm his body from the inside while we warm it from the outside. When he is awake, it is imperative that he has hot broth as well as hot tea. That way he will regain his strength quickly."

Gwain began to moan and Davida knew she needed to attend to both of his feet as well as his other hand. She also knew that once he was awake, he would be in considerable pain. She recalled her teacher saying that the boys with frostbite would have a sensation not unlike having needles stuck in their skin. "He is in pain," Charles observed.

"It is expected. He will be in pain for several hours, if not days. At least we were able to treat him quickly. His skin color is returning nicely. We will keep bathing his hands, feet, and face. With the dumping of each basin of used water, we will use water that is just a bit warmer until he is no longer chilled. I have also told Emma to bring some hot tea and force him to drink it. Thank goodness he was close enough to home that none of you suffered from frostbite in your attempt to find him."

"Would you have been as concerned about the rest of us as you are about Gwain?" Charles asked, just loud enough that only she could hear.

She quickly turned to face him. "What a terrible question for you to ask. This clan is my family now. It wouldn't matter who was suffering. I could care for any member of this household in the same manner. You must think me a horrible person if you even consider I would not have compassion for any one of them." Tears formed in her eyes, not because of what had happened to the man she had come to love, but because of her husband's hurtful words.

To Davida's surprise, Charles enfolded her in his arms. For the first time since the men brought Gwain into the great hall, Davida gave into the stress and tensions. With gentleness she didn't know Charles possessed, he led her to the bed.

"You have told everyone what to do, but you are exhausted. It is evident you didn't sleep last night. Tell me what must be done next and I will see that it is done. It is important for you to rest."

"But Gwain will need the bed."

Charles looked across the expanse of the oversized bed. "There is enough room. Now what do we need to do next?"

"Keep bathing his hands and feet as I have instructed until the blisters are formed. Once you see one forming on whatever area is affected, apply the same ointment that would be used for kitchen burns. When that is done, wrap the area in clean linen. When it is no longer necessary to bathe his hands, dress him in a warm nightshirt and bring him to bed. When you do, make certain he is covered so that the heat from the blankets can seep into his body. Once all that is done, there is nothing more to do but wait until he wakes up on his own."

She suppressed a yawn as Charles left her side and went to get a warm blanket from his own bedchamber. She hardly remembered closing her eyes. Above the sound of the people who were attending to Gwain, she began to dream of a time when she would be big with Gwain's child. *"I will find a way for the two of us to be together,"* the Gwain in her dream promised.

The words echoed in her subconscious until she drifted into a much deeper sleep.

Chapter Eleven

Gwain pulled himself from the depths of sleep only to wish he was still oblivious to what was going on around him. His hands and feet felt as though they were being stung by hundreds of bees. He tried to flex his fingers, but his hands wouldn't move. It seemed as though someone had bound them with strips of cloth.

With great effort, he opened his eyes. It was evident he slept in Davida's bedchamber. To his surprise the room was illuminated with many candles, leading him to believe that it was late into the winter evening.

Beside the bed, he saw Charles dozing in one of the chairs that usually sat in front of the fireplace. Next to him, Davida's even breathing told him she was asleep. If that was the case, why was Charles sleeping in a chair as though he was watching over the two of them?

As he stared at Charles, his brother opened his eyes. An uncharacteristic smile crossed his lips. "We have been worried about you," Charles said, his voice hardly more than a whisper.

"What happened?" Gwain asked, forcing the words past his lips. The throbbing of his head brought back memories of the old crone and the story she'd told him about Davida. He also remembered falling from his horse, embracing the warm bliss of unconsciousness that replaced the biting cold of the wind. As the thoughts crowded, he realized he could use his fall as a reason not to disclose everything that had happened and that he had learned. He could tell Charles a believable half-truth while reserving the rest for Davida's ears alone.

"We found you riding close to the manor house after you were gone all night. Where were you?"

"We argued," Gwain began. He pretended to have trouble remembering what happened next. "I rode out without giving thought to the storm. When it got worse, I took refuge in the woodcutter's cottage. I..."

"Gwain! Are you awake?" Davida asked, her voice heavy with sleep. "Why didn't you wake me, Charles?"

"You needed your rest," Charles replied.

Davida threw off the covers. To Gwain's dismay, she was fully dressed, her heavy dress was one he had seen her wear many mornings.

"What I need is to prepare fresh tea and broth, as well as check on his hands and feet."

It surprised Gwain when Charles got up from his chair and started to leave the room.

"You're right, of course," Charles said, as he continued toward the door. "I will go to the kitchen. I am certain Briana will know what you need."

Gwain watched Charles leave the room and debated as to how much he should tell Davida in his brother's absence.

As though unaware that Charles had left the room, Davida lifted the covers from Gwain's body. Even though he was in pain, his cock didn't seem to be affected. Just the touch of her hands as she unwrapped the bindings caused his cock to come alive.

"The salve is working," Davida declared. "I must remember to thank Emma for her expertise with such things."

Even though his hands and feet were in pain, he couldn't help teasing Davida. "Something else is working as well." He watched as she glanced toward his unruly cock.

"It's best if you restrain yourself in that part of your body. Since you saw fit to stay away all night, you've frozen your hands and feet. I hope she was well worth it."

The idea that Davida thought he was with another woman was intriguing. How could she think that he would desire anyone after being in bed with her? Knowing that the reason for his pain was frostbite was another matter. Perhaps it was best if he told her the truth.

"I was with another woman." Before he could continue, tears

87

formed in her eyes and he wanted to take her in his arms and tell her everything. Before he could begin to explain, Charles and Briana entered the room with hot tea and broth.

"Make certain he eats all of it," Davida said, as she turned from him and hurried toward the door.

He watched as Charles followed her. This wasn't what he wanted. He wanted to be alone with Davida and tell her what the old woman had told him. To his dismay it would be Charles who would comfort her.

"What did you say to her?" Briana asked, her tone one of accusation rather than concern.

"For some reason, she thought I was with another woman." He could feel his strength waning but he needed to continue. "When she asked the question, I merely confirmed her suspicions. You and Charles came in before I could explain. I understand why my hands are bound, but why does everyone look like I've returned from the dead?"

"Because you have. This morning, Davida was sick with worry because you did not return last night. When the men brought you to the great hall more dead than alive, she knew exactly what to do. Had she not stopped Charles, he would have plunged your frozen hands into hot water. She said it would have done more damage than good. We could all see that she was drained as she attended to you relentlessly, but it was Charles who finally insisted she rest. It was evident she did not sleep at all while you were gone. Are you so blind that you do not know she has fallen in love with you? How could you be so cruel as to actually tell her you were with another woman?"

Gwain stared at his sister. The pain in his hands and feet, no matter how severe, was not as bad as the one in his heart. He had not meant to upset Davida. Had Charles and Briana not returned, he would have told her of the old woman and the incredible story she told him while they were snowbound.

* * * *

Davida would have given anything to be able to lock herself in her bedroom, turn on *Law and Order,* and forget everything that had happened in the past two days.

"Davida, please wait up."

She knew someone followed her, but she hadn't turned to see who it was until Charles called her name and asked her to stop. "Why? Why should I stop, Charles?" she asked as she whirled around to face him. "You want me only as a baby factory so that I can give you a son. Gwain only wants me because I spread my legs and give him a good fuck. What do I get out of it? You are my husband in name only because there is another who satisfies you sexually. Gwain is my lover, but he spent the night with another woman. I have a husband and a lover, but I spent last night satisfying myself, and today I cared for him in an attempt to save his hands and feet. It would have been better if I'd allowed you to plunge his hands and feet into hot water. It would have served him right if even one of his injured parts had turned black and fallen off." She knew she bordered on hysteria, but she didn't care. Someone had to tell these idiots what life was really like for her.

Charles' strong hand clasping her shoulders brought her back from the brink of total despair. "It is a strange situation into which I have brought you, but we have all come to love you. Gwain loves you as a desirable woman who has become very important to him. I love you as I have always loved you. I have dreamed of you since your naming day, only to have my ability to love you stolen from me by the war I had to fight against the English to save my country. Your exhaustion has overcome your reason where any of us are concerned."

"What does exhaustion or even reason have to do with Gwain spending the night with another woman?"

"Before you awoke, he told me that he had ridden away from the manor in anger, paying no attention to the weather. When the storm hit, he took refuge in the woodcutter's cottage. I have been told that people have seen an old crone living there. It is entirely possible that she gave him refuge for the night. It would explain why he told you he was with another woman. Unfortunately he did not get the opportunity to finish what he was saying, for Briana and I came into the room. Give him a chance to explain further. I am certain you will realize that you are the woman he wants to be with sexually as well as emotionally."

Davida thought of Gwain's erection while she tended to his hands. His cock had become hard and stood at attention under the covers. At the time she had teased him about it, but she realized it was her touch that

89

had made him hard. He did desire her, but did he love her?

"Come back to your bedchamber and talk to him. You will see that he did not betray you for another."

She allowed Charles to guide her back down the long hallway. As she did, she couldn't help but remember the twinkle in Gwain's eyes when he told her about the other woman. Could it be that he had been teasing her? She hoped so. The thought of another woman allowing him to sink his cock deep inside her and drain him of his life-giving sperm made her angry. She cursed her jealously. She had never been jealous of Fred, but of course he never gave her cause.

When they entered the room, Briana met them. "I gave him as much of the broth as he would take, but he went back to sleep. I also told him he was being cruel to you. I know when my husband beds another wench, but not because he tells me. It's a shame that the cold only froze his hands. If you ask me, it should have taken his cock as well as his balls."

"Do not be so harsh, sister," Charles said. "We only know that he became lost in the storm. It was God's will that the old crone who has taken up residence in the woodcutter's cottage took him in. I had planned to ride out there and make her leave, but the storm kept me here. Had I driven her off, as I had planned, Gwain could be dead by now."

Davida cursed her hasty accusations, even if they were only within her mind. The thought of Gwain dying because of the storm caused her to begin to cry.

"It is best if you do not spend the night in this room," Charles said. "You need time to rest. Brian will stay with Gwain while you sleep in my chamber. I want to be able to keep watch over you."

"And what else do you plan to do to me?" she asked, unable to suppress the question that burned on her tongue and sounded so terrible.

"Only to make you comfortable. It has been a long day and one which none of us will soon forget or forgive."

She allowed him to take her to his bedchamber. After he spoke a few words to Brian, the younger man left the room. To her surprise, a fresh nightdress lay on the bed. It was evident that Charles had planned this all along.

Charles helped her with the fastenings of her dress and when she stood naked in front of him, he dropped the nightdress over her head. The warmth of the garment was a welcome relief from the chill of the room against her bare skin.

"It would be easy for me to take this time to enjoy your body, but it would be wrong to do so without being able to give you the pleasure you so deserve. I will be content to hold you until you have fallen asleep."

She looked at him in saddened surprise. How many times had she heard Fred say the same thing? He'd suffered from erectile dysfunction. The doctor had prescribed the pump and something called "muse," but neither had been completely satisfying. The pump had been painful to use and the drug had left him with a burning sensation. When they tried Viagra, it didn't have the effect they had hoped for and made him sick to his stomach. In the end, it was best if she used her battery-operated vibrator to give her relief. It was better than seeing the distressed look on Fred's face.

She couldn't help but wonder if Charles' problem was a cause of war or nothing more than erectile dysfunction. If she had some of Fred's Viagra, she could certainly find out quickly enough.

Before she had a chance to think on it further, Charles led her to the bed and helped her to slide under the covers. She watched as he undressed. He didn't seem to be ashamed to do so in full view of her. As he did, she saw a jagged scar that ran from his waist to his groin. Following its line, she saw his cock lying limp in its nest of red hair. If the injury had not occurred, he would have been the one in her bed, the one giving her not only satisfaction, but also a child.

When he finished putting on his nightshirt, he crawled into bed beside her. He immediately took her in his arms. Being so close, without the benefit of the heavy clothes the two of them wore during the day, made her throb with desire.

As though he sensed her need, he pulled her into a tighter embrace. "I do want you, Davida, but I do not take you to my bed to fuck you. That is why my brother resides in this house. I will only comfort you and allow you the rest you need."

Davida nodded and closed her eyes. After laying her head against his chest, she drifted off to sleep listening to the cadence of the beating of his heart.

Chapter Twelve

Gwain awoke to the realization that the tingling in his hands and feet had subsided. He lay with his eyes closed for a moment. The sound of even breathing told him that someone was in the room with him, but who? It certainly wasn't Davida. He knew the sound of her breathing when she was asleep. It had to be a man, for it was deeper.

Cautiously, he opened his eyes and looked toward the chair beside the bed. He was surprised to see Brian sitting in the chair where Charles had sat the day before.

"I see you are finally awake," Brian said. "I will go down to the kitchen and instruct them to send up your morning meal."

Before he could get to his feet, Gwain reached out and touched his arm. "Where is Davida?"

"It is possible that she is still sleeping."

Gwain looked to the empty place beside him in the bed.

"She did not sleep in this room. After the way you treated her, she spent the night with Charles."

The thought of his brother sharing the delights that he knew no other but he had shared made him sick with jealousy. *How could she so easily give herself to Charles when she knows how I feel about her?*

You know the answer. You told her you spent the night away from the manor with another woman. Had Briana and Charles not come into the room when they did, you could have explained everything to her. Now you will have to make her listen to what you have to say.

Across the room he heard the door open. "Is he awake?" Davida whispered. Her voice made his cock stir with desire.

92

"He just woke up. I was going down to the kitchen to request that his breakfast be sent up. Do you want to go instead?"

"No, I'll stay here. You go down and tell the women to bring up breakfast for both of us, then go and take your rest. I know it has been a long night."

Brian left the room and Gwain watched as Davida crossed the room to sit in the chair Brian had occupied earlier.

"How are you feeling this morning?" she asked. Her voice sounded with both concern and hurt that he knew would not soon go away.

"The tingling is gone. About what I said yesterday…"

"You spoke the truth. It shouldn't bother me. I have no exclusive claim to you."

"Please don't interrupt me. Yes, I was with another woman. Several days ago, when I went to the stable to see to my horse, I found an old hag waiting for me. She told me that she was a soothsayer and that she had something to tell me about you." He saw her face go white at his words, but continued on. "I asked her what it was and she told me to meet her at the woodcutter's cottage. When I left the manor, I could tell that there was snow in the clouds, but I was afraid not to go to her, since she had been adamant about both the time and the place where I was to meet her."

A knock at the door interrupted his narrative. He watched as Davida took a deep breath before going to open the door for whoever had brought the breakfast tray. He could tell that she was shaken by what he told her. It was evident that she would confirm everything the old woman told him.

"You should eat while the porridge is still hot. I am certain the rest of your story can wait until your belly is full."

"Then you believe me?"

Davida nodded. "It is evident that you believe what the old woman told you. That being the case…"

"Are you from the future? Are you…"

"We will talk of this further once you have eaten and I have checked your hands and feet."

He knew better than to argue with her. She had drawn the battle lines in the scrimmage. Just the few words she'd spoken confirmed his

93

suspicions, and if he wanted to learn more he knew it would be by allowing her to set the pace of things.

As though she were feeding a helpless baby, she spooned the porridge that had been soaked in rich cream into his mouth. He had to admit it tasted good and took care of the gnawing hunger that plagued him.

When his bowl was finally empty, she ate her own meal. He delighted in watching how her delicate mouth opened just wide enough to allow the spoon to enter and deliver the food to her. He wished it were his cock that was filling her mouth and not a spoon filled with porridge.

She lingered over the meal before turning her attention to his hands and feet. The words burned on his tongue and he longed to continue telling her all that the old woman said, but she had made it quite clear that she would hear none of it until she finished the tasks she had told him about earlier.

As she took the wrappings off his hands and feet, he could feel the coolness of the air against his skin. From the table beside the bed, she picked up a jar of the ointment he remembered Emma using the night before. He half cringed as he remembered the pain involved when the old woman rubbed it into his skin. Instead, the ointment had a soothing effect.

"Your blisters are healing very well. I think it is best if we leave them uncovered. It is also best if you rub your hands and feet with this ointment often. It will keep the skin…" she stopped as though searching for the correct word.

"If you cannot think of the correct word, use one that you remember from your life in the future."

A half smile came to her lips. "The word I was looking for was supple, meaning soft and pliable, like well-tanned leather. You know that in order for it to be soft, it must be worked with special chemicals."

"I understand completely. Do I have your permission to continue telling you what the old woman said to me while you work?"

"Perhaps that would be best. I shudder to think of what she said."

"She told me that Davida, the woman who Charles had been promised to, came to her on the eve of her wedding to Robert. She wanted to be told of a happy future. Instead, she was told that Charles

94

would come to claim her and slay Robert in the process. The lass was indeed young and untried, and she loved Robert with all her heart. She could not stand the thought of being bedded by anyone but him."

"Not even you, with the expertise that you possess?"

"Before the old woman could tell her of me, she begged to change places with a future incarnation in order to avoid the humiliation of having to bed the man who killed her one true love. That is why..."

"That is why you came to me on the Ouija board. It was to soften the blow of waking up in this time in a body that certainly didn't belong to me."

"I do not understand. What is this Ouija board that you speak of?"

Davida began to laugh. "In the early twentieth century a board was devised as a psychic game. People believed that the spirits could come from beyond the grave to communicate with them through the board. On the morning before I changed places with Davida, my friend and I were playing. We did so often for fun, but never took any stock in it. I was surprised when it spelled out your name and then told me that I had been your lover in 1470 and that I was your brother's wife. While I was sleeping, I had a dream about Robert and Davida. In it they were in a meadow and he was preparing to take her as you have taken me. It was so erotic that I awoke with an ache that no one other than myself could ease. When I reached down to fulfill my passion, I realized that nothing about the body I found myself in was normal. I had switched places with Davida. That is why I was unsure how to answer you when you asked if I was a virgin. If my dream was indeed true, Robert had already taken that which I gave to you."

"This future you speak of is fascinating. I want you to tell me more."

"In time. For now, I will finish with your hands and feet and then pay close attention to the other part of your body that needs me."

"Are you saying that you want to be fucked?"

"I doubt that you are strong enough for that, but I do want to make certain that your marvelous cock and balls have not suffered from the cold. It would be a shame if I removed these covers to find them blistered. If that were the case, how could you ever satisfy me?"

"Are you telling me that my brother did not satisfy you last night when you were in his bed?"

Tears formed in Davida's eyes. "Charles is a magnificent man. He has the build most men would kill to have, but when he undressed in front of me, I saw his cock lying limp and no bigger than that of a young boy. He could never satisfy me. Just seeing him without benefit of clothing made me feel sorry for him. It is a good thing that he has Brian to see to his needs."

"I have been meaning to ask you why my brother's liaison with Brian does not bother you."

Before she answered, she pulled the covers back completely and began to examine his cock. Her touch made him come to full attention. She ran her hand over the entire length of his hard shaft and then pumped against it with one hand while she fondled his balls with the other. When he thought he could stand the pleasure no more, she positioned herself between his legs and began to gently suck on his balls while still manipulating his cock with her hand.

"What are you doing to me, woman?"

"Just showing you a few of the tricks I brought with me from the twenty-first century. Considering that you know my secret, I am certain we will find many ways to be more creative in our lovemaking. I have read every erotic book I could get my hands on but never thought I would be able to act out my fantasies. At first I was annoyed with the woman who so easily took over my body, to say nothing of the comforts of the twenty-first century. Now I realize that I have been given a second chance at love. Let me show you ways that I can give you pleasure without exhausting you. Once you are completely healed, I will tell you of other positions that I am certain you will find satisfying."

Gwain relaxed. He was more than ready to have Davida relieve the ache in his cock. He knew he would prefer sinking it deep within her velvety depths, but since she was intent upon sucking him dry, he wouldn't complain.

* * * *

Davida had been horrified by the fact that Gwain knew about her trip through time to grace his bed. Even so, she mustered all of her composure not to let him know. At least with the truth out in the open, she could use some of the things she had only read about without him wondering how she had learned such tricks.

The fact that he relaxed meant that he was intrigued by the possibility of bedding a time traveler rather than horrified to think that his bed partner was, in reality, someone who had lived a full life.

With him completely relaxed, with the exception of his cock that stood at attention, she got to her knees and straddled him. As she slipped his hard shaft into her cunt, she moaned with the pleasure that she had so missed during their time apart.

"Oh!" the word exploded from his lips as though he was taken completely by surprise by her actions.

She knew he had expected her to take him in her mouth, but this was far better. She had to admit she enjoyed the taste of his cum as it slid down her throat, but she found much more pleasure when it filled her cunt and sent life-giving sperm to the innermost regions of her womanhood.

As she moved up and down on his cock, she contracted and relaxed the muscles of her vagina in order to give him the most pleasure possible. In doing so, she felt herself cum several times in rapid succession before he finally reached his brink and spilled his seed into her body.

This is the dream of every woman who has passed her prime. To be able to make love to a man and actually experience an orgasm at my age, at least my age in the twenty-first century, is beyond description.

When the last shudders of ecstasy stopped, Davida reluctantly pulled herself from his cock. "I hope that helped to hasten your healing," she said, as she crossed to the fireplace to dip one of the love clothes into the water that was warmed by the fire.

"I am certain I will be able to make love to you sooner than you think. That does not say that I objected to you making love to me."

After washing the remnants of their love from the insides of her legs, she took a fresh cloth and washed his cock and balls. "This is one practice that I certainly wish would have lasted through the years. In the future, men are not so considerate as to cleanse their lovers. The most Fred ever did for me was to cover me up when he was done."

At the mention of Fred, she saw Gwain tense. "The old woman told me that you were a widow. Would you tell me of your husband?"

"If that is what you'd like."

"I want to know everything there is to know about you. What the old woman told me makes so many of the things you have said and done make sense."

"Then I will tell you of a time when men are not considerate and love is so free that everyone speaks of it even in mixed company. It will make for a good topic of conversation while I give you your bath."

A wicked smile crossed Gwain's lips. "Do you intend to carry me to the tub?"

"Of course not. I will give you a bath, as you lay in this bed. The soles of your feet are still blistered, so walking will be difficult for you. Give me a minute to prepare your bath and then we will begin."

She returned to the hearth for towels, soft cloths, soap, and a basin of water. *What will I tell him? How will I make him understand that all the wonders of the twenty-first century pale in light of being in his arms?*

"Which time period do you like the best?" he asked before she could decide where to begin.

"Both have their merits. For the creature comforts, I would say the twenty-first century. For the joy of being with you, I would choose the time I am now enjoying."

"What are these creature comforts you speak of?"

Before she spoke, she sat the basin down on the table and dipped the cloth into the water in order to produce a rich lather with the soap. "In my time, houses are always either warm in the winter or cool in the summer. It's called central heat and air conditioning. Our food is cooked on stoves rather than over an open flame, and we have a wonderful invention called a microwave that cooks the breast of a chicken in less time than it takes to put it on the spit in the kitchen. We do not travel by horseback, and the trip that took so long from my uncle's home to here would take less than half a day. There is also a device that brings news into your home from anywhere in the world as it is happening. If there is a war, you are able to view it from the comfort of your living room."

Gwain wrinkled his nose. "Why would anyone want to watch men being killed in battle?"

Davida thought for a moment before answering. "Perhaps for the same reason the ancient Romans went to see the Christians torn apart by lions or medieval folk watched jousting matches. If I can believe what I am told, many people gathered in London to watch as William Wallace was executed."

"How do you know of Wallace?"

"This is going to be hard for you to understand. Have you ever seen a play?"

Gwain nodded.

"In my time, plays are made into what are called movies. They are played in theatres all over the world so that people can see actors depicting famous characters from history, or other stories that they are interested in seeing. One of my favorite movies is *Braveheart*. It is the story of William Wallace. The horror of war that the people of Scotland endured is far beyond understanding."

"Wallace was a brave man, indeed. I have heard many stories of his exploits in his bid to free Scotland from British rule. Although it is fascinating, it is not history that I want to hear, but stories of the future." When he finished, he yawned broadly.

"I will tell you anything you want to know, but for now you must rest. I fear the exertion has been too much for you. We will surely continue our discussion once you are rested. Perhaps by tomorrow you may even be healed enough to come to the great hall for your meals."

As soon as she spoke the words, another thought crossed her mind. If Gwain were well enough to be with the clan, would he be anxious to tell all of how she came to be in the body of a much younger woman?

"Your eyes are very expressive, my love," Gwain said. "If you think I will betray the truth about you to the rest of the clan, you are mistaken. The words the old woman told me were for my ears and my ears alone. They were not meant to be spread like idle gossip. I never intended to tell anyone but you of what she said. Your secret is safe with me."

"Thank you," she whispered, as she fought both the tears that threatened to spill from her eyes as well as the smile that crossed her lips.

Chapter Thirteen

The bright sunlight in the room signaled to Gwain that it was late afternoon. Since Davida's bedchamber was on the west side of the manor, the bright rays of the sun did not cross the floor until after the midday meal. When he opened his eyes, he saw Charles sitting beside his bed.

"I am pleased to see that you are finally awake, brother," Charles greeted him. "Brian told me that you slept throughout the night, and now I have seen for myself that you have slept away the day. What could you have possibly done that was so exhausting?"

Gwain thought of the way Davida had made love to him hours earlier. It wouldn't do for Charles to know that they had enjoyed each other by the light of day when he had been adamant that they should do so only during the hours of darkness.

"It must be that my injuries require me to sleep more than usual," he replied, hoping that the words would be ones that Charles would not question.

"I saw Davida when she returned to the kitchen with the tray that was sent up for your morning meal. She had the look of a lass who was well-fucked. How did you manage such a fete in your condition?"

Gwain laughed. "There is not much that escapes your view, brother. If you must know, Davida brought me to arousal and rode me as you would ride a new stallion. She did the work and I merely reaped the benefits. The woman is a delight in bed, but of course she graced your bed last night and you certainly must have..."

"I allowed her to rest and nothing more. How can there be anything more when I am no larger than a boy? She stirred me so that I wanted her to suck my cock and manipulate my balls, but I had nothing to give her in return. At least with Brian, I am able to give him pleasure without the expectation of me fucking him. She is a delightful lass, but once she has a child, she will no longer expect a nightly fucking. Then and only then will she be content to be my wife."

Gwain agreed. If he could believe the old woman, once Davida delivered a son to Charles, she would return to her own time and the woman who belonged in her exquisite body would come back. Since she had fled her time and body to avoid marital relations with Charles, it would be possible that she would be content to live a life not unlike that of a Catholic nun.

"Davida told me that when you awoke, I was to help you apply the ointment to your hands and feet. She is convinced that if the treatment continues throughout the day you should be able to return to the great hall and all those who are concerned with your well being."

Charles handed the ointment pot to Gwain after dipping his fingers into it so that he could massage Gwain's feet.

"I know we have never been close, but can I ask you a question?" Gwain inquired as he rubbed the ointment onto his hands.

"We are brothers, born of the same parents to the same clan. You can ask me anything."

"Is it your injury that keeps you from bedding Davida, or are you in love with Brian?"

Charles looked up, startled at the question Gwain posed. "At first it was the injury that made me realize that Davida would never be satisfied with me, but when Brian came into my life, I found that I did have a deep affection for him."

"That is good. I would hate to think that you use him only for sexual satisfaction. Has he ever sucked your balls?"

"Sucked my balls?" Charles questioned as he looked up from his task. The expression on his face was the answer that Gwain was looking for. "I have never heard of any such thing being done."

"Then you are missing a great pleasure. Davida has sucked my balls until I thought I could stand it no longer. That was how our lovemaking began this morning. She sucked my balls and I thought she would do the

101

same to my cock. She has done that before and sucked me dry. After such an oral fucking, one is unlikely to soon recover. It is one of the most stimulating things I have ever encountered."

The shocked expression on Charles' face turned to one of a man intrigued by an exciting new idea. "Perhaps when Brian returns to my bed this evening, I will have something new to show him. The idea is fascinating, to say the least. As for you, I have a feeling that Davida is in for a treat as well. It is evident that you are more than ready to fuck her in a more conventional way."

Charles glanced down at the nightshirt that now stood as though someone had erected a tent beneath it. "It is evident that your desire has not become frozen, as were your hands and feet. It should be an interesting evening for both of us."

* * * *

"Tell me more about the future," Gwain said as soon as Davida entered the room.

"What do you want to know?"

"The old woman told me you were a widow and were well past the age where you could be called a maiden or even a young woman. Why not start there?"

He watched as she sat down in the chair next to the bed. As much as he wanted to take her as he had in the past, he needed to know about this part of her life as well. He could wait to make love to her.

"In the twenty-first century, the year is 2013. In the spring I will be fifty-nine. I was married when I was very young, but my husband and I were unable to have children. I don't know which of us was to blame, but I do know that I missed being a mother. My husband's name was Fred and he was not exactly interested in what you would call bed sport. He preferred to do things the same way time after time until he was no longer able to perform. Then he did agree to give me pleasure with what we called a hand job. I also had a dildo to take away the loneliness. Out of desperation, I watched lots of porno flicks."

"What are they?"

"I told you about movies. Well, those are movies depicting men and women making love in various positions. In one film, the woman actually has sex with three guys at the same time."

"How is that possible?"

"One did it from behind in the place where men make love to men, one did it in front, and the third, well, she did him with her mouth, much as I have done you. I learned a lot from watching them, as well as reading erotic books."

"You have mentioned reading in the past. Do all women in your time read?"

"Boys and girls alike are taught to read. Some women even go on to be lawyers, doctors, and ministers in their churches. It is a very different time."

"You said people are freer in their lovemaking? How is that so? Do men and women bring extra partners into the marriage bed?"

Davida laughed at his question. "Not exactly. Marriage is still sacred, but girls are not expected to be virgins on their wedding night. Many times men and women live together and never marry. They even have children and sometimes other partners."

"Was that the way it was in your marriage?"

A sly smile crossed her lips. "I was raised in the fifties and sixties when young women were not as promiscuous as they are now. When I was in school I was expected to be a good little girl and be a virgin on my wedding night, just like all of my friends. Of course I wasn't, and neither were many of my friends. A lot of the girls were having sex with their boyfriends and were married less than nine months before their first child was born. Back then you had two options, marry the boy even if he didn't want to be married, or give your child up for adoption."

"Did you have sex before you married Fred?"

"I did. I was fifteen and we did it in the backseat of his car. That's the means of transportation about which I told you. It was exciting and the thought of getting caught made it even more so. I thought the excitement would continue, but unfortunately he turned out to be disappointing in bed. Don't get me wrong, I loved him with all my heart, but I would have liked a relationship like the one I've had with you. It's what makes a marriage."

"How will you cope once the baby is gone and so am I?'

"I will plead with Charles to allow me a lover. If that doesn't work,

I'm already proficient at masturbation. It's highly likely that if I ask Emma she'll be able to find me a dildo of some sort."

Gwain laughed at her statement. She wouldn't have to find a dildo. There was one waiting for her in the twenty-first century. Once her child was born and named, she would be returning to the life she had lived with all the creature comforts of which she has spoken. He would be but a delightful memory, if she remembered him at all. He needed to make the most of what time they had together.

"I have had enough of this talk. I want you in my bed. Tonight I will make love to you in any way you desire. Just tell me what to do and I will try to mimic those movies of which you speak."

"Are you sure you're up to this?"

"I know I am. What delights do you have in store for me tonight?"

"First, I must undress and you must take off that ridiculous nightshirt. There must be nothing between us to take away from our pleasure. You go first, and I will give you a treat by doing a striptease for you."

"A what?"

"In my time, women take off their clothes in a sensuous way so that men will give them money. In most of these places, they do not make love to the men, only leave them so horny that they will either visit a prostitute or go home and fuck their wives for an entire night. Are you ready?"

Gwain lifted his ass from the bed so that he could easily remove his nightshirt. Once free of the linen garment, he sat up against the pillows, eager to see this thing that Davida called a striptease.

Slowly she unhooked the fastening of the bodice of her gown and allowed it to slip off her shoulders. Once she was free of it, her breasts strained against the undergarment that hid them from his view. Only a slender ribbon held the garment in place. Instead of untying it, she finished removing her skirt until she had on only her drawers. He knew nothing hid her cunt except the fabric that covered it, as most women preferred the ease of a split crotch.

He could feel his cock grow hard with desire, but she stood too far away from him to touch her and pull her onto the bed.

Once she stepped out of her dress, she slowly untied the ribbon, exposing her breasts for his scrutiny. Once they were free, the nipples puckered in the chill of the room. She threw back her head and took a breast in each hand, playing with the nipples until his hands itched to do the same. Soft mews, like a contented kitten, passed her lips as the pleasure she was giving herself manifested itself verbally.

As though she knew he was getting excited, she dropped her hand to the opening in her drawers and slipped her finger into her cunt. He could smell the musk of her sex and when she withdrew her finger, she stuck it in her mouth and licked her essence from it.

His own mouth watered with excitement, as he could almost taste her on his tongue. When she again put her fingers into the crevice, she massaged herself, bringing tears of expectation to his eyes. Again she withdrew her fingers and instead of sucking on them, she put them to his lips. He mimicked her actions by taking them into his mouth and licking her delightful wetness from them.

"Take off your drawers," he ordered. "Can't you see that I want you more than I have ever wanted you in the past?"

"That was the general idea, but tonight you must play by my rules."

She took off her drawers and stood before him, allowing him to play with her clit and put his fingers inside her until he knew she was as ready for sex as he was. Instead of straddling him, she went around to the other side of the bed and got on her hands and knees.

"Do you want me to fuck you in the ass?" he asked, bewildered by her actions.

"No, my love. I think you will find fucking me from behind in the proper place much more satisfying for both of us. Now, get on your knees behind me and hold onto my tits while you sink your shaft deep inside me."

He was surprised at how easily he was able to access her from this position. He shoved his cock further into her cunt than ever before and the sensation was exciting. His balls banged against her ass, giving him additional pleasure while his hands manipulated her ample breasts.

When he finished, they both lay on the bed exhausted and ready for sleep. Again she got up and retrieved the soft cloth, in order to cleanse their bodies.

"You are indeed a magnificent lover," he said once she returned to the bed so that he could pull her into his arms.

"It's easy to be a good lover when your partner is as anxious to please you as you are to please him."

"Was Fred anxious to please you?"

"In his own way. When he couldn't perform he obliged me, even though I know it broke his heart to do so. He wanted to make love to me, but he was in a position not unlike that Charles finds himself imprisoned in."

Her statement bothered him. "Was he injured in a war as was Charles?"

"Perhaps it would have been better if that had been the case. He was the victim of his own body. He had a disease called diabetes as well as another called high blood pressure. The two diseases, combined with the medication needed to keep him stable, robbed him of his sexual desire. It was hard for me to stop having sex when I was but forty-three years old."

"If I do my calculations properly, that means you have not enjoyed a sexual relationship for more than fifteen years. How could you abide it?"

"Had it not been for the sex toys I indulged myself with and the fact that I learned to give myself satisfaction, it would have been impossible. I rarely let Fred know of my disappointment, though. I loved him far too much to humiliate him in such a way."

Gwain pondered her words. Would he ever expect a woman to give up what was so natural because of her love for him? Charles expected it because he didn't understand women, but Gwain knew that women were as excited by the sexual act as men, that is, if they were introduced to it in the proper way.

"He must have been very special for you to give up so much because of your love. There are few who would go without rather than humiliate the one they love."

Her soft, even breathing told him she had not heard his last words. He pulled her closer and held her protectively until he too joined her in sleep.

Chapter Fourteen

Davida was late in getting her period. Without a calendar, she couldn't be certain just how late she was but she knew it had been more than four weeks since her last period. Emma had said nothing, and Davida hadn't brought up the subject either. She wanted to be certain before she said anything to the older woman.

It was easy to recall the number of times that she'd jumped to the conclusion she was pregnant only to find that she was mistaken. The one that stood out in her mind the most was when Fred was in a car accident and she had stayed by his bedside in the hospital for days on end. She was so late she had called her doctor and made an appointment, and then woke on the morning of the scheduled visit to find she had her period. It would be the same now. The scare with Gwain and his frostbite was enough to throw her off schedule.

She missed not having him in her bed when she woke up in the morning, but it was to be expected as they continued the charade that Charles was the one in her bed. As soon as her feet hit the floor, she had an overwhelming need to barf. Without even grabbing the wrapper from the end of the bed, she rushed to the chamber pot to empty the contents of her stomach.

This must be morning sickness. I am pregnant. Am I happy or sad? If I'm pregnant and the child is a boy, I will lose Gwain.

Once she finished puking, she rinsed her mouth with water from the receptacle beside the fireplace. She wished it was ice water but knew that was another thing she'd left behind in the future.

Her stomach settled and the thought of being pregnant brought to

107

mind all the disappointments she and Fred had suffered. Every time her friend Sue got pregnant, she said she hated the first three months. She would go on to describe being sick in great detail until Denise wanted to cry. It seemed all Sue had to do was have her husband hang his pants on the bedpost and she'd get pregnant. At least that's what all the girls in the office said.

The fact that the morning sickness passed so quickly surprised Davida. Instead of returning to bed, she dressed for the day and went down to the great hall for breakfast. To her surprise, she was suddenly ravenous.

As she went down the stairs, she nodded a morning greeting to the members of the clan who only weeks earlier had been strangers. Even Ian looked more presentable now that they were no longer on the road and he had taken the time to clean himself up.

"You look radiant this morning," Charles observed.

"Thank you, Charles. I feel radiant. If I am not mistaken, Christmas is fast approaching and I am in the mood to decorate the hall."

Charles laughed at her statement. "Briana said the same thing this morning and ordered her husband and Gwain to go out into the forest in search of the Yule log."

"Can we also have a Christmas tree as well as pine boughs? I so love the smell of pine."

"A Christmas tree? What kind of a tree is that?"

Davida knew she had again spoken out of turn. These people probably didn't have a tree nor did they have ornaments stored away in the basement. "It is a pine tree that is cut down and brought into the house. It's a tradition that was carried out in my uncle's house. Of course, we do not have any ornaments with which to decorate it. It would be foolish to bring such a thing in from the forest. Instead, I would like just a few pine boughs so that their scent can fill the hall."

"I do think such a tree would be impractical, but I will ask Gwain to bring you pine boughs if that is what you desire."

"Oh, thank you, Charles," she said, as she put her arms around his neck and gave him a kiss of gratitude.

* * * *

108

Gwain saw Davida kiss Charles. Even though he was secure in her love for him, he couldn't help the feeling of jealousy that clutched at his mind as well as his heart. He wanted her kisses to be for him and him alone.

You are being a fool. Once your son is born and named, you will no longer be welcome in this manor. Davida will be lost to you. For all intents and purposes, she will be Charles' wife and you will return to your uncle's estates to claim that which has been promised to you.

"I need to speak to you, Gwain."

The sound of Charles' voice summoning him to the high table silenced the voice of reason that insisted upon sounding in his head. The thought of being so close to Davida by the light of day made going to where she sat a pleasure rather than a chore.

"What do you require of me, Charles?"

"It is not my desire, but that of my wife. Davida wants pine boughs brought into the hall. She had requested a tree, but it seems a waste to bring a live tree inside."

"Perhaps it is a tradition that she remembers from her life before she came to us. I know it is a tradition within the estates of our uncle. I remember fondly having a tree at Christmastime. I especially enjoyed decorating it. We always put a star at the very top. It was one that the cook made out of cookie dough. Once the twelfth day of Christmas ended, she took that star, along with the other ornaments that she had made, and brought them outside to feed to the birds. It seemed only fitting that the birds should enjoy the same Christmas cheer as the rest of us."

He watched Davida intently. It was possible that the tradition of the Christmas tree had survived into the future from which she had come.

"Then we shall have a Christmas tree. I will order the women to begin making these ornaments as you call them. Will you be able to tell them what they need to do, Davida?"

"I've never supervised the actual making of the ornaments, but I think I can help. I also think that the children would be able to help me as well."

"Good," Gwain replied. "I will look for the perfect tree as well as some pine boughs. In our uncle's home we always used garlands of dried heather. I know the women often dry it to use in tea or medicines. I think enough could be found to make garlands for the tree. This will be a very special Christmas indeed."

* * * *

Davida spent the rest of the day in the kitchen overseeing the baking of Christmas cookies for decorations. She'd made her sugar cookies so many times in the past, it was easy to duplicate the recipe using honey instead of sugar. The women were amazed when she insisted they roll the dough thin and cut out shapes of stars, trees, and bells before putting them into the oven to bake.

She kept a close eye on the cookies and when they were done to her specifications, she made certain they were removed promptly so they wouldn't burn. As much as she wanted to put powdered sugar frosting on them, she knew these people wouldn't have the ingredients necessary to make the sweet confection. Instead, she beat several eggs in a bowl and then brushed them lightly over the tops of each cookie. Since no one would be eating her creations other than the squirrels and the birds, it didn't matter that the eggs were uncooked and could cause salmonella.

By evening, the tree graced the center of the great hall and at her instruction stood in order for the branches to drop naturally. The children had been busy as well. During the fall, they had collected pinecones and nuts and were busy, under Gwain's supervision, making them into ornaments to grace the tree.

It was evident that all the holiday festivities were not to Charles' liking, but he said nothing. Instead, he indulged her in the preparations that made her so happy.

By the time evening came, Davida was exhausted. After eating supper with Charles, she retired to her bedchamber. She didn't have to wait long for Gwain to join her.

"I'm pleased that the tradition of the Christmas tree has survived throughout time. Will you tell me of your other Christmas traditions?"

"Only if you hurry to get into this bed with me." She enjoyed watching Gwain as he prepared for bed. She knew it was something she would never forget, even when he was banished from her bed. With luck, his son would grow up to be as magnificent a man as his father.

As soon as he crawled beneath the covers and took her in his arms, he urged her to begin telling him of Christmas in the twenty-first century.

"When I was a little girl, we lived on a farm and I was an only child. My mother always insisted on putting up the tree on the first of December. She said we were Advent people rather than Christmas people. It was always decorated with store-bought ornaments that were glass and of various colors. Strings of lights were also added to the tree. Of course it was a *real* tree."

"What other kind of tree is there but a real tree?"

Davida laughed. About fifty years before I came to this time, people decided they wanted trees that didn't dry out and make a mess. The first ones were made of metal and were really ugly. In later years, they were made out of an artificial material and looked as real as any tree from the forest."

"Did you have such a tree?"

"Guilty as charged. I was the one who always had to clean up the mess, and considering the needles were usually imbedded in my carpet, I enjoy having the artificial tree. Of course, there are still a lot of people who spend exorbitant amounts of money for real trees every year. Last year, I saw that trees on the lots were going for more than I had spent for the tree that I am able to use year after year. With the forest land disappearing, it's a shame to cut down the trees. Even though I know that the trees are grown on tree farms for this purpose, I still think it's a waste."

"What do you mean the forests are gone?"

"The population of the world is growing so quickly that the forests are being cleared to make way for new homes. The people have used the wood for fires to heat their homes and cook their food, without replenishing that which they have taken."

"Then how do you heat your homes?"

"If my geography is correct, we are not far from the North Shore of Scotland. In my time there will be offshore drilling for oil, which will be used to heat our homes and cook our food. It is all too complicated to try to explain." She stifled a yawn and snuggled closer to Gwain. I would much rather make love to you than to try to explain everything about the

111

future."

He reached up to caress her breast. As soon as his hand touched her sensitive nipple, she flinched in pain.

"Did I hurt you?"

"Not really. My nipples are extremely tender tonight."

He pulled aside the covers and examined her bare breasts. "Are you with child?"

His question took her by surprise. "How did you know?"

"You forget that I was trained to give pleasure to women. I was also trained as to what happens to a woman when she is with child. Her breasts become tender and the nipples change color, as yours have. Just the thought that you carry my child brings tears of joy to my eyes."

"I too have shed tears, both the joy and sadness. I told you that Fred and I were unable to have children and so I am savoring every moment of this pregnancy. On the other hand, I know that once the child is born and named, you will no longer be with me. The thought is one that sobers and saddens me."

"Then we will make the most of the time we have together." He kissed her before making slow delicious love to her. When they finished, she snuggled closer into his arms and fell into a sleep filled with pleasant dreams of babies and the man she knew she loved more than she ever thought possible.

* * * *

By Christmas morning, Davida had piled presents high beneath the Christmas tree that had graced the great hall for so long. Ever since her arrival, she had been knitting. She found she enjoyed making mittens for the children. No child was missed and as she finished, she asked Gwain to print the name of a child on each package. It was something she could have done herself but knew that if she did, it would create more questions about her past that she wanted no one but Gwain to know about.

She had spent hours in the kitchen helping with the preparations for Christmas dinner, adding her own touches to several of the dishes that were being prepared. She also worked in private, making warm socks for Gwain, as well as a beautifully embroidered shirt for Charles. She wished the shirt could have been for Gwain, but her gift for him had to be in secret. As for Briana, she made her a set of delicately embroidered handkerchiefs.

All of the preparations reminded her of the hours she used to spend making sweaters for each of her nieces and nephews for Christmas, as well as the hand-crocheted doilies that she made for her sisters-in-law and friends. Those were fond memories. She decided that over the winter she would approach Ian, who she had heard did some excellent carving and ask him to make her a crochet hook. By this time next year, she would be able to make doilies if she could remember the pattern. If nothing else, she could always revert to the granny square and elaborate on it a bit to make it delicate.

After midnight Mass, said by Father John, Davida asked Gwain to help her bring the packages for the children down to be placed under the tree. He hadn't asked questions, but had joined her early the next morning to watch the children as they were given their gifts.

When they had first awakened, she had given Gwain her gift.

"But I got you nothing," he protested.

"You've given me the greatest gift of all," she countered, placing her hand over her still flat belly. "Even though we will not be together, I will always have a piece of you to hold close to my heart."

She recalled the conversation as one by one the children came into the hall and gasped in amazement at the packages that were meant for them.

"What is all this?" Charles asked when he joined them.

"Christmas is for children," Davida replied. "Didn't God give us a gift on that first Christmas? He gave us his son and since then people have given gifts in remembrance of that time. At least that is the story that was told in my uncle's household."

Charles put his arm around her shoulder and gave her a reassuring hug. I think that is a wonderful tradition. The children love to receive gifts. When will they be able to open them?"

"I have asked Gwain to distribute them when the children are all assembled. In the meantime, I have a gift for you."

"For me? But I am not a child."

"No, but you are my husband. You deserve to be remembered on

Christmas as well."

"Did you also remember Gwain?"

She nodded. "And Briana, too."

She took the gift for him from the chair where she had set it earlier. Her heart beat in anticipation as she watched him open it. The shirt was white and the embroidery was of the same colors as the plaid that denoted the McGowan clan.

"But I have no gift for you," Charles lamented.

"Gwain said the same thing, but indeed you have given me a gift, the great gift of allowing me to get to know Gwain. In turn, he has also given you a gift." For the second time in but a few hours, she put her hand over her belly.

"Are you with child? Do you carry my son?"

"Yes, I am with child, but whether the babe is a boy or a girl will not be determined until the day of its birth. For now, it is enough that this precious gift grows within the confines of my womb."

Charles took her in his arms and kissed her as though he had been the one to plant the child beneath her breast. Before he could make any announcement to the clan, the children were clamoring to receive their gifts.

Everyone watched as each child opened their packages and squealed with delight over the warm mittens that would grace their hands throughout the winter.

"There is one more gift that Davida has given the clan," Charles declared as he held up his hands for silence. "By this time next year, she will give me a child. Even now it grows beneath her breast. Praise be to God for gifting us with this child."

A cheer went up from those gathered, and Father John came up to the high table in order to bless both Davida and the child.

Chapter Fifteen

The winter was indeed long and Gwain filled their nights with delightful lovemaking. When Davida became large with child in the summer, she assured him that sex would not harm the child. It was only Charles' concerned reaction that kept Gwain from enjoying her delights on a nightly basis. Instead, he was content to enfold her in his arms and love her with touches and kisses.

"Why is it that you no longer make love to me?" she asked, as they cuddled one warm summer evening.

"Charles is afraid it will harm the child."

"What does Charles know? In my time, women have sex right up until the time of delivery and it doesn't harm them one bit."

"So you have said, but I want to take no chances with this child. It is too important to my brother, and I would not risk you having to take the brunt of his wrath if something were to go wrong because of our lovemaking."

"But don't you realize that once the child is born we will not be together again?"

Tears were rolling down her cheeks as they did every time they talked of the future and what the birth of a son would mean to them.

"Perhaps the child will be a girl and we can start all over again." He knew he didn't mean it. The soothsayer had told him that the child would be a boy. She also said that before his naming day Davida would return to the future and the woman who had not wanted to make love to Charles would again inhabit her body and raise the child.

"Not the way this kid kicks. I know he's going to be a linebacker for

115

the Green Bay Packers."

Gwain laughed at her referral to the future. "Not in this time. You forget you are not in the future that you left behind. I understand what you are saying, though, as you have often told me of this magical place called Green Bay and this wonderful game of football the people of the future so enjoy."

"I am so glad that you know my secret. At least when things like that pop out of my mouth you understand. I have to be so careful of what I say to Charles. At times I think he considers me to be daft."

"I doubt that he considers you daft. If he were to know that you had changed places with his bride-to-be because she did not want to take him to her bed, he would be angry. It is best that we allow his anger to remain hidden beneath the surface of his being."

Davida agreed and allowed him to caress her. As he did, he thought of a way he could make love to her without doing harm to the child.

"Turn your back to me," he instructed.

"Are you planning something wicked?"

"I plan to make love to you one last time, for I too believe the child is a boy."

Once her back was to him, he slid his fingers into her from the back, while massaging her clit. When she was ready for him, he made love to her very gently from behind as he had done when she had been on her knees so many months earlier. He was careful only to penetrate far enough so that he could give her pleasure without causing harm to the child.

Even though their lovemaking was unconventional, it was delightful and it produced a memory that would last him for the rest of his life. Never again would he love a woman in the same way he had loved Davida. The thought was sobering, to say the least, and brought tears of frustration to his eyes. His brother had no idea whatsoever what he had in this woman. He only hoped she would remember him once she returned to her own time, and that those memories would be fond ones.

* * *

Davida awoke to the first cramps of labor. Earlier, she had heard Gwain leave her bedchamber. She would have to make her way down to the main hall and summon Emma to come and help her with the birth.

The moment her feet hit the floor Davida felt her water break and the warm fluid gush toward the mat that covered the stone floor of her chamber. Before she could dwell on the necessity of replacing the mat, Briana entered the chamber.

"It is so late that Charles was worried about why you had not come down to share the morning meal with him."

As soon as she saw Davida standing in the puddle of water, Briana hurried to her side. "I see there is good reason for your absence. How long have you been experiencing the pains?"

"They just started."

"Once we get you into a clean gown, I will go down and bring Emma so that she can give you some tea to ease the pain you will be feeling."

"Please, Briana, please don't let her give me the tea until I ask for it. I want nothing to dull the pain, for I fear this is the only time I will give life to a child."

"What nonsense...of course, if the child is a boy Gwain will be banned from the manor house. I will see to it that Emma abides by your wishes."

The second labor pain hit with a vengeance, causing Davida to realize that the pains were no more than five minutes apart. Tears stung her eyes as she urged Briana to hurry in, fetching the midwife.

* * * *

Gwain watched as Charles said something that sent Briana toward the stairs. "Where is Briana going?" he asked when he made his way to his brother's side.

"I am concerned about Davida. She has not come down for the morning meal."

"She is close to her time. It is possible that she is still asleep. I have noticed that she has problems walking and seems to be very tired."

"Is it the child that tires her or her lover? I would be a fool if I did not realize that you spend your nights in her bedchamber."

"And if you weren't so blind you would see that she is in need of comfort. It is not for my satisfaction that I spend my nights where I do. It is because I know she needs the comfort of being held and told she is

117

beautiful. Her body is swollen with the babe and she needs reassurance. Of course I am certain that is something that escapes you since you are well satisfied and assured at night."

"What the two of you need is to put this argument to rest," Angus said as he joined them. "The entire clan knows of your dislike for one another. Do not let them know why, although most have already guessed the reason you brought Gwain back to the manor. Gwain is right, the lass does need the comfort of her husband's arms, but day by day it is evident that you are more devoted to Brian than to her. It is a shame, for she is a beautiful and loving girl."

Before either Gwain or Charles could answer their uncle, Briana hurried down the stairs.

"Where are you going?" Charles demanded.

"I go to fetch Emma. The babe is about to be born and from the way this has started, I do not think it will be a long process. It is possible that by nightfall the next head of the McGowan clan will be born."

Gwain cringed. His time with Davida was quickly coming to a close. If the babe was indeed a boy, he would be leaving this manor never to return, and Davida would be returning to her own time. He wondered if the woman who took her place would be as loving as the one who had stolen his heart.

"You are right, Uncle. I think it is best if I go to my chamber and start packing my belongings. I too think the child will be a boy and my work here will be ended. I cannot shake the dust of this manor from my shoes quickly enough."

He knew his words sounded angry, he meant them to. If he never saw Charles again, it would be soon enough. As for his son, as much as he wanted to raise him, he knew that would be impossible. Charles would be, for all intents and purposes, the boy's father. He would never know the part Gwain had played in his conception. The thought of Charles raising the child to be an exact copy of himself sickened Gwain. The boy would learn of war and killing rather than the ways to love a woman. He could only pray that the Davida who would become his mother would teach him a softer way of life.

"It is not wise for you to go to your chamber at this time," Angus warned. "All know that it adjoins Davida's chamber, and men are not welcome in the birthing room."

Defeated, Gwain turned on his heels and left the hall. Outside, the heat of the morning was already beginning to build. Above him, the bright blue of the summer sky promised another hot day.

He thought of going directly to the stable, but decided it would be best if he walked off his anger. Heading out toward the moors, he walked without purpose, trying to decide what his life would be like without Davida. To his surprise, the old woman he had met in the woodcutter's cottage so long ago appeared ahead of him.

"The lass is giving birth to your son," she greeted him. "Why is it that you are out here alone instead of in the hall gloating over your child?"

"You know the answer to that. I am not welcome to share the joy of this day. That is for Charles and Charles alone. As soon as the priest is summoned and the boy is named, I will leave and never see anyone from this manor again. Even today Charles berated me for spending my nights in Davida's bed. It is not as though we were making love. I stayed there only to give her comfort and to tell her how much I love her. Once I am gone, there will be no one to do these things for her."

"You forget, once you are gone, she will also return to her own time. The woman who will take her place will know all that has transpired and the part you played in it, but she will not be the woman you love. The Davida who will be within the body you so love will be content to spend her days raising her son and not having to share her bed with the man who claims her as wife."

"What will the woman I love remember of this?"

"For her it will be a delightful dream, one which will not fade from her memory. As Denise, she will continue on as she had before. Her husband is gone and after the dream of being in your arms, none will ever tempt her again."

"When we talked before, you told me that it might be possible for me to travel through time and be with her."

"It is possible and I could do it, but think of what you are asking. You are a young man, barely 24 years of age. If you go to her time, you would have to do so as a man of her own age. You would be nearing the end of your life. The best I could promise you would be ten years, if not twenty. Do you want to give up so much of your life for a woman? Think on this long and hard before you come to any decisions regarding this matter. Once you do, I will be near and will sense your need of me. Now it is time for you to return to the manor house, for Emma is about to bring your son down from the upper chamber so that both you and your brother will be able to see the next clan leader for the first time."

Gwain nodded and turned back toward the manor. When he again looked back, the old woman had disappeared as quickly as she had appeared. He shook his head and wondered if he had imagined the entire conversation.

* * * *

"I can see the head of the babe," Emma declared. "One more push and the shoulders should be out. Then, just one more push and you will see the child you have only felt within your belly for so very long."

Two more pushes, just two more pushes. If this child is a boy it will mean that I will never see Gwain again. Will I be able to live without him in my life? Will I be content to have a life without love?

The urge to push silenced the voice that sounded within the confines of her mind. "Good job, lassie," Emma's voice sounded above the screams that tore from Davida's throat. "One more, just one more, and the babe will be born."

The lusty cries of a child ready to meet the world and begin its life echoed off the walls, as Davida gave one last push.

"It's a boy!" Emma declared. "This child is not only a boy, but a healthy one at that. In all my days of delivering babies, I have never heard of one so anxious to greet the world. I can tell he is healthy because of the way he was crying before he was ever completely out of his mother's body. As for being a fit leader for the McGowan clan, one but has to look at his manly attributes to see that he is hung as well as the stallion that Charles gave to Gwain. Many generations of McGowan babies will spring from his cock when he is old enough to plant it within the folds of the lass who will be his wife.

Unless he is injured as was Charles, and then who will father these future generations? It is certain I will never have another son, so there will be no brother to bring to this manor to plant the seed. No matter whom this child calls father, it is undeniable that he belongs to Gwain. Even now, I can see the resemblance. Everything about him screams that Gwain is his father.

Chapter Sixteen

From the preparations in the great hall, it was evident to Gwain that Father John had arrived to officiate over the naming and christening of Charles' son. Gwain had only seen the boy once and that had been on the day he was born, but his lusty cries alerted everyone in the manor house to his presence.

Today, he would see Davida and his son for the last time. As soon as the boy was named and properly christened, Gwain would leave McGowan Manor. He longed to see Davida again as well as hold his son, as would be his duty as Godfather. The memory of this day was one that would have to last him for the rest of his life.

"Gwain, it's good to see you again. I was afraid you had already gone back to your uncle's estate," Father John greeted him.

"I felt it my obligation to remain here until my brother's son has had his naming day. That was our agreement when I came here two years ago. Besides, how could I be the Godfather to my nephew if I did not stay?"

"And what have Charles and Davida decided to name the child?"

"Charles told me they have decided to keep it a secret until the ceremony. I can say that he is a lusty lad and I am told he has a fine head of red hair. He is definitely a McGowan."

A commotion from behind them caused Gwain to turn toward the staircase. Once he did, he saw Davida coming down, carrying the infant in her arms with Charles by her side. As soon as he saw her he knew that the swap had been made, and the woman he loved no longer inhabited the body of the woman on the stairs.

122

Charles motioned for Gwain to join them and even allowed him the privilege of holding his son. Together, the four of them approached the priest while the members of the clan hushed their conversations and turned their attention to the ceremony that was about to take place. Once they stood in front of Father John, Briana also joined them.

"What is the name you have chosen for this child?" Father John asked, his booming voice filling the hall.

"He is to be named for the great hero from Scottish history, William Wallace McGowan."

Gwain listened to no more of the proceedings that went on around him. The name that was given to his son was the one that he and Davida had so lovingly chosen. It was evident that Davida had told Charles what she wanted to name the boy before she was returned to the future.

"The name ye have chosen is fitting for the lad," Angus declared. His words made Gwain aware of the fact that the ceremony had ended. "I did not think you were so well versed in Scottish history."

"You underestimate me, Uncle," Charles replied. "I have heard of Wallace, for his name was whispered among the ranks of those with whom I served. He was a great hero. To my delight, Davida had heard of him as well and decided that a bonnie lad like this deserved a hero's name."

As though he agreed, William made his presence known. As he did, Gwain looked down on the screaming infant that he held in his arms. The lad's face was red from crying and his red hair attested to the temper he would one day possess.

I pray you will grow to be as understanding as your mother, as brave as the man you call father, and as considerate a lover as I am. I will not see you again, but I will always remember you as my son.

* * * *

The journey from McGowan Manor to the estates that would someday belong to Gwain was bittersweet. He hated leaving behind the son he had created with Davida, and yet to stay would have been fruitless. He could never again love Davida, for the woman he loved resided far in the future.

Ahead of him he saw the familiar boundaries of the Fletcher Estates.

123

As he neared the manor house, he saw a rider coming toward him.

"Gwain, can that be you, lad?" his Uncle Keith asked as he rode closer to him.

"Yes, Uncle, it is I. The deed is done. Charles has his son and I am no longer welcome at McGowan Manor."

"Then the time is finally right for that which must be done. I will make arrangements for your name to be changed to Fletcher. In that way, the final ties to those bastards who took my sister from me will be cut. When that is done, I will turn the management of Fletcher Manor over to you."

Gwain knew that this had been his uncle's plan from the beginning, but cringed at the prospect. "The trip has been a long one, Uncle Keith. I would appreciate a hot bath and some of your fine scotch whiskey. When we are comfortable, there is much I need to tell you."

Keith nodded and led the way back to the house. Once they entered the great hall, he began to bark orders to the servants and the hall became alive with people running to do his bidding.

As Gwain washed the dust from his body, he thought of the day he had washed the same Scottish dust from Davida. She had been frightened and alone in a strange place and he had felt the sexual pull between the two of them as soon as he touched her woman's soul.

"May I help you, Gwain?" Athena asked as she entered his chamber.

"If only you could, Athena, my love."

"Is that to mean that the lass Charles had you bed was pleasing to you?"

"More than pleasing. She has spoiled me for any other woman who may ever enter my life"

"Are you telling me you fell in love with her? I thought I taught you better than that."

"There was no way that I couldn't fall in love with her. She was the perfection of womanhood and she taught me games I never dreamed possible. Together we produced a perfect son and she insisted that he be named William Wallace McGowan."

"I see. It is a shame that you will not grace my bed this night. I have thought of little else than the feel of your hard cock within me, but I do understand. In time you will need me. It was the same for me when I fell

124

in love with the man who first purchased me. When I was taken from his household, I thought I would never again be able to bed another. Once the ache in my cunt overcame that in my heart, I was able to love again. It will be the same with you. I am a patient woman. When you are ready to take me to your bed, I will be here for you."

"What of Uncle Keith?"

"He satisfies me, but you must know I have always had other lovers, just as he has had other lovers. The bonds of marriage hold neither of us. With your Aunt Katie being gone for so many years, your uncle has not lived the life of a priest. We understand each other. You, too, will come to understand that you cannot stop being a man just because the great love of your life is lost to you."

Athena plunged her hands into the hot water and began to wash Gwain's back. Once she finished, she washed his chest and cock as well. The way it sprung to life was embarrassing to Gwain. It made him feel as though he was being disloyal to Davida.

"I told you that you are still a man in every sense of the word. I will be waiting whenever you want me."

His need of her was stronger than his vow to remain celibate. As soon as he was out of the tub, he took her to his bed. The foreplay that he had enjoyed with Davida was not necessary here. Athena knew what he needed and was ready to fuck him without the niceties demanded by a woman in love.

When he spilled his seed into her body, she took him in her arms and pressed his lips to her nipples. He suckled her as his son was surely suckling Davida. The fact that the act brought tears to his eyes made him realize what decision must be made about his future.

"You are as good as you ever were," Athena declared when he washed away his essence from her cunt and clit. "Even so, I am afraid there is something missing."

"What do you mean?"

"You spoke of your love for your brother's wife. It still burns brightly within your body. That is why there was no love play between the two of us. She must have been quite a woman to capture your heart so completely. I envy her. Now, return to this bed and take your rest. Your uncle has instructed me to see to your needs and make certain you rest. The trip from McGowan Manor is a long and tiring one. He wants you to be fresh for supper this evening."

Obediently, Gwain crawled back into bed and allowed Athena to hold him until he fell into a restless sleep that was filled with dreams.

"I didn't want to leave you, Gwain," the Davida in his dream declared. *"I had no more control over returning to my own time than I did when I was brought here. I will never forget the son that the two of us created. Although the same McGowan blood flows through his veins as it does through Charles' veins, he belongs solely to you. I am certain he will do you proud."*

The dream faded and Gwain drifted into a deeper, more restful sleep.

* * * *

Supper in the Fletcher household was, as always, a festive affair. Rather than the high table at his brother's manor, Gwain enjoyed the fact that the long dining table that Keith insisted upon using was filled with all the members of his extended family.

The food was exceptional and prepared to perfection, the wine was the very best available, and the conversation centered on what had happened since Gwain left to do his brother's bidding. With the meal finished, Gwain and Keith adjourned to the library for a glass of whiskey.

"Now, lad, tell me what weighs so heavily upon your mind," Keith said, once they were seated in the fine leather chairs that graced the book-lined room.

"It is your intention that I become your son in every sense of the word. Before I left for McGowan Manor, I looked forward to this day. Now I cannot accept that which, at one time, would have made me so happy."

"Why not?"

"You know why Charles summoned me to his household. It is true that he has a man as a lover, and that his injury has left him little bigger than an untried boy. It was my duty to bed his wife and give him his son, but of course you know all of that. What you don't know is that I have fallen hopelessly in love with my brother's wife. It is best for both of us is I leave Scotland, for to remain here would be too difficult."

"And what would you have me do with my estates? To whom would I leave them?"

"Your oldest daughter Morna has two sons. The youngest of the boys will have no inheritance from his father. You are still a young man. Offer to foster the boy as you did me and tell Morna that he will be your heir. In that way, he will be able to take over your estates when you are gone."

"But what of you? I love you as I would have loved my own son. How can you give up your inheritance?"

Gwain thought for a moment. For his plan to work, he would have to have the money to do so.

"I ask only for the funds to begin a new life."

"Then whatever you wish will be yours. Do you want jewels or gold? No, don't answer that question. You will have both. I have more of both than I will ever need. I will give you half of my accumulated fortune and wish you well. I know wherever you settle you will prosper. Athena has told me of your great love for the woman Charles calls wife."

"And you understand?"

"Of course I do. You never knew your Aunt Katie, but she was my great love. I thought I would never love again when she died giving me our last daughter. Of course, the pain eases. In my dreams she has given me her blessing and I have found love as well as enjoyment in Athena's arms, to say nothing of the other lasses who willingly share my bed. It will be the same for you. Time heals all and you will again be able to love without the hurt of knowing the woman is not Davida."

Gwain thanked his uncle. "I will stay the week and then I will be on my way."

"Where will you go?"

"I do not know. What I can tell you is that I will be as far away from Scotland and Charles as I can get."

Chapter Seventeen

Denise awoke, the dream she had experienced still vivid in her mind. She knew that dreams only lasted a few minutes at the most, but this one had gone on for what seemed like months.

The bright sunlight told her she was in her own room and her own bed. A check of her body told her she was Denise, saggy boobs, flabby stomach, and all. The man who had invaded her Ouija board, Gwain, was but a dream and probably never existed.

Without dwelling further on the dream that had seemed so real, she got up and made her way to the bathroom. The sparkling fixtures of the room seemed almost alien. As her bottom caressed the padded seat of her toilet, she felt as though it had been months since she experienced anything this luxurious.

Once she finished, she turned on the water in the shower. After adjusting the temperature and changing the spray from a fine mist to a pulsing jet, she stepped into the stall and allowed the water to cascade over her body. As she did, she glanced through the steamy glass doors and into the mirror that hung above the sink. In it she saw first the distorted reflection of her fifty-something body and then the body of Davida, the young woman from her dream.

It wasn't a dream, Denise. You gave me the son I wanted and now I have returned to my own time, as you have returned to yours. Your life was far too fast-paced for me. I will never forget what you, as well as the soothsayer have done for me. My only regret is not knowing Gwain in the way that you did. He seemed like a good man when he acted as the

128

Godfather for my son, William Wallace McGowan.

The voice that sounded within her mind faded away, as did the reflection in the mirror. She again saw her naked body with all its bumps and bulges.

Could it be true? Did I change places with Davida and enjoy the delightful nights of lovemaking with Gwain?

With no answers forthcoming, she finished her shower and washed her hair. After wrapping herself in a fluffy towel and drying her hair, she went into the bedroom to find something to put on for the day.

Before she had a chance to pull on her jeans, the phone rang. "Hello," she answered, knowing full well that Lydia would be on the other end of the line.

"Where have you been? I've been worried sick. I've been calling for three days and getting no answers."

"Oh, Lydia, you wouldn't believe me if I told you. Give me a couple of minutes to get dressed and then come over. Have I got a story to tell you."

Denise hung up the phone, pulled on her jeans, and found a sweatshirt that would be comfortable for the mid-November day. She had just finished brushing her hair when the doorbell rang.

"This better be good," Lydia greeted her. "I've been out of my mind with worry over you. I'd decided that if I didn't get an answer today I was calling the police to see if you'd died over here."

"It's not that dramatic," Denise assured her. "Let me put on a pot of coffee. I think we're going to need it."

Once they were seated at the kitchen table, Denise began. "Do you remember when we were playing Ouija the other day and Gwain invaded the board?"

"How could I forget it? That was one of the most frightening things I've ever seen."

"It was more than frightening. The next morning I woke up in 1470 and found myself in the midst of the most erotic story I'd ever heard of. Gwain was…"

She paused to ponder the memory of Gwain's lovemaking and to mourn her loss at returning to the twenty-first century, over five hundred years away from the man she had come to love.

Once she regained her composure, she related the story to Lydia.

"That had to be some dream. It's no wonder you slept for three days."

"I don't think it was a dream. This morning I heard Davida's voice in my head while I was showering. She thanked me for giving her a son to love. I was so intrigued that I went to the computer and did a search for William Wallace McGowan. It brought up several sights. The one I found the most intriguing I left up on the screen so that we could read it together.

Lydia stared at her in disbelief. "There really was a William Wallace McGowan?"

"It looks that way."

Together they went into the office and Denise brought the computer to life. The article she read earlier was still on the screen.

> *William Wallace McGowan was born in 1471, the son of Charles McGowan. When William was but five years of age, his father, Charles, was killed by his friend, Brian Graham. In retaliation, Angus McGowan, Charles' uncle, killed Brian and took on the task of raising William.*
>
> *At the age of twenty-six, William entered politics and along with running McGowan Manor, was a well-known man in parliament. His fame spread as far as London and Paris and he served for awhile as a diplomat to France.*
>
> *Having fathered six children, it is rumored that he was an exceptional lover who outlived two wives. He also cared for his mother, Davida, until her death in 1506.*

"If I'm not mistaken, he was his father's son in every way," Denise said.

"Why don't we go in and see if we can contact him again on the Ouija board. Maybe he wants you back."

"Let me rest up from the last time," Denise replied before they both dissolved into laughter.

They were interrupted by the ringing of the phone. Denise let it ring twice before she answered so that she could compose herself. "Hello."

"Denise, this is Sue. Is Lydia there with you? I couldn't get an answer at her house."

"Of course she is. Do you want to talk to her?"

"I want to talk to both of you. I'm in charge of the dance at the Senior Citizen Center tomorrow afternoon and I need the two of you to say you'll come."

"You've got to be kidding. The last time you dragged us to one of those dances, Wally Anderson drooled all over my shoulder. I don't think I'm ready for another round with that old fart."

"Please, for me. Two of the girls who usually come are in the hospital and I'm always scrambling for women. For some reason this town has more old men than it does old women."

"Thanks for the compliment."

"You know what I mean. Please come. I really need you."

"Well, give me a minute to talk to Lydia."

Denise put her hand over the receiver and turned to her friend. "What do you think?"

"About the same thing as you, but why not? What else do we have to do tomorrow afternoon? With any luck, Wally won't be there. It could prove interesting."

Denise nodded. At least it would take her mind off Gwain and the lovemaking they had enjoyed when she had traveled back into time. "Okay, Sue, but this is just for you. If Wally Anderson so much as looks my way, I'm out of there."

"Not to worry. His kids put him in a home last week. I doubt that he'll be there. I heard there's a new guy in town and I talked Tom Janish into bringing him."

"New guy? How new can he be if he's able to attend the dances at the senior center?"

"New as in he just moved here. Give it a shot. What have you got to lose?"

"Nothing, I guess. We'll see you tomorrow afternoon at two."

Denise hung up the phone. "How do I let her talk me into things like this?"

"The same way I do. Yesterday when I went down there I got

131

suckered into playing in a euchre tournament."

"You were there yesterday?"

"Well, you weren't answering your phone, at least, the 'you' who was here wasn't answering so I thought what the hell."

"Then you knew about this dance."

"The dance is a standing thing. I told Sue yesterday that we weren't interested, but she kept insisting. I thought by coming over here I could avoid her call. Guess I was wrong. What are you going to wear?"

"Wear? I hadn't given it much thought. I guess that purple skirt and winter white top and shrug I got on sale last spring would do."

"Not only would that do, but it would get those old men's juices flowing. You could get lucky and one of the younger ones might just follow you home. I certainly don't have anything that sexy. Do you mind if I raid your closet?"

"Not at all. I have an outfit that might just get you a man in your bed tomorrow as well."

Lydia laughed. "I don't know about that. At my age, I think I'd be like the dog that finally catches the car he's been chasing for years. Once I had it I wouldn't know what to do with it."

"Don't sell yourself short. If my memory is right, I had no trouble doing it with Gwain back in 1470."

* * * *

Denise didn't know exactly why she took such care in dressing for the dance at the Senior Citizen Center. She knew all the old men who went there and she knew there wasn't one of them who deserved the view down the front of her top.

She finished putting on her makeup just as the doorbell rang. Before going to answer it, she slipped into her new pumps and grabbed her winter coat from the hall closet.

"Are you ready to rumba?" Lydia asked.

"As ready as I'll ever be. How did that dress fit you?"

Lydia stepped into the warmth of the house and opened her coat. Beneath it, the burnt orange dress hugged her curves better than it ever did for Denise.

"Whoa, talk about a knockout. I think that dress definitely belongs in your closet rather than mine. I think I only wore it once and then I looked like someone had stuffed a sack of lumpy potatoes into it."

"You're exaggerating, but I do love this dress. I agree, the color wasn't quite right for you, but it does suit me quite well."

They were still laughing when they made their way to Lydia's car. With the cold snap, she had started it before coming across the driveway to get Denise.

"I feel like a lamb being led to the slaughter," Denise remarked, as they pulled out of the driveway. "If I ever let Sue talk me into something like this again, please give me a good swift kick where it would do the most good."

"I promise, but I have a feeling today will be better than the last time we tried this. Who knows, this new guy might turn out to be Prince Charming and sweep you off your feet."

"I doubt it, but as we always say, nothing ventured, nothing gained."

The Senior Citizen Center sat at the end of Main Street and the sign in the lobby said that the dance would be held in the second floor ballroom.

"Do you remember when this building was the library?" Lydia asked as they took the elevator to the second floor.

"I sure do. Fred and I made out a lot in the stacks. I wonder if now that it's the ballroom I'll get lucky again."

The elevator doors opened and they stepped into the hallway leading to the ballroom. As she remembered from the last time she had come to the dance, the room was decorated in much the same way they used to decorate the gym at the high school for the prom. Streamers were hung from the ceiling and a bandstand, complete with antiquated record player, was set up at the far end of the room. As they had before the mirrors that lined all the walls for the aerobics classes reflected every move the dancers made.

"You did make it," Sue exclaimed as she came to greet them. "I was afraid you'd back out at the last minute."

Denise studied Sue's appearance while Lydia made small talk with their friend. She recognized the dress that Sue wore as the one she bought fifteen years ago when her husband, Alex, was made president of the Elks Club. As a matter of fact, it was probably the same dress she wore to every one of these dances. Of course, it really didn't matter. These guys were all so old they probably couldn't remember if they gummed down oatmeal or cream of wheat for breakfast.

"You're just in time," Sue continued, unaware of Denise's scrutiny. "We're about to begin and the stag line is bigger than usual. I'm really glad the two of you came. At least we'll have enough partners for everyone."

Denise glanced toward the line of men waiting to dance. At least Wally wasn't there. After hanging up her coat, she was surprised when someone tapped her on the shoulder.

She turned and gasped. If she didn't know better she would have thought an older version of Gwain stood there. She swallowed hard and smiled sweetly.

"My name is Denise," she said, extending her hand.

The man took her hand and brought it to his lips. "I know. My name is Gwain and I knew you in 1470. You were my brother's wife and I was your lover."

She allowed him to continue to hold her hand as she fought the urge to swoon into his arms. "But how? Why?"

"Davida was not the only one who knew the soothsayer. She did everything in her power to keep me from trying to follow you to this marvelous time. It took almost a year, but I finally convinced her that I would rather spend a limited time with you than a lifetime without you. The inheritance from my Uncle Keith has made me a very wealthy man and as such, I plan to spend whatever time granted us in your bed, that is, if you will have me."

There were no words to express her feelings. Even if there were, she couldn't get them past the lump in her throat. Instead, with tears rolling down her cheeks, she embraced him. "Yes," she finally whispered, "yes my love. I am forever and always yours to love. Now, for appearances sake, we have to have at least one or two dances before we steal away to somewhere more private."

About the Author

Mild Mannered wife, mother and grandmother by day, Shari Dare spends her nights writing and writing and writing. Having been inspired by an English assignment in her sophomore year of high school, she had never quite finished the assignment. New stories pop into her head every day with never enough time to write them all.

A Wisconsin native, she grew up a country girl, but enjoys her "city" home. She and her husband of over 50 years, Bob, live in a mid-sized town close to the Illinois border. Deeming Bob "A Saint" for putting up with her she has never regretted marrying her high school sweetheart just two days after graduation in 1964.

http://www.derr-wille.com

Other Books by the author with Melange

Man in the Forest
Black Conley

Coming Soon

Seeking SirGwain